# Dan

MW00917607

## By Zoe Chant

# Green Valley Shifters

This is book one of the Green Valley Shifters series. All of my books are stand-alones (they never have cliffhangers!) and can be read independently, but characters do recur. This is the order the series may be most enjoyed:

Dancing Bearfoot (Book 1)
The Tiger Next Door (Book 2)
Dandelion Spring (Book 3)
Bearly Together (Book 4)
*Broken Lynx (forthcoming)*
*A Green Valley Christmas (forthcoming)*
*Lion in Wait (forthcoming)*

# Chapter One

L ee lay awake for a long moment without opening his eyes, not ready to be awake, and not sure why he was.

"Someone is watching us," his bear supplied, wary and grouchy.

Lee opened his eyes at last, and found the cause of his uneasy feeling staring at him across the empty spread of bed. Blue eyes that matched his own were framed with white-blonde curls that were nothing like his own dark locks.

"I start preschool today," Clara told him, matter-of-factly. "I dressed myself. But I couldn't tie my shoes." The offending shoes, a worn pair of sneakers with pink cartoon bears, were laying on the bed between them. The knotted laces showed her efforts.

Lee groaned, and looked at the clock on the bedside table. "It's five in the morning," he explained.

"I don't want to be late."

Lee refrained from trying to explain details about time to a four-year-old, and resigned himself to getting up. He snagged a pair of pants from a moving box and padded barefoot across the thick carpet to sweep Clara up and toss her effortlessly onto the wide bed while he got dressed.

She giggled and tumbled, then sat up seriously. "Will my new teacher like me?" she asked anxiously.

"You don't need to worry about that, cub!" Lee was quick to assure her. "You're going to have a great time. Aunt Bella says it's the best school in the whole town."

Like the concept of time, it was pointless to add that the entire town was only thirteen hundred people strong, and there had not been a choice at all. If the preschool did not work out, he could pack them back up and move them to another town, but Lee was weary of moving, and tired of cities. He already loved the house they had found, and the quaint little town of Green Valley. His bear loved the wilderness that was only a short wander out his backdoor. If the preschool didn't work out, maybe he would just hire another nanny and keep Clara home. He was suddenly hopeful that his daughter wouldn't get along with the teacher.

"Would you like a special breakfast?" he offered, to distract her. "You can help me wash dishes, afterward."

Clara's face lit up. "Yes! Pancakes! With blueberries! Can I make the bubbles for the dishes?"

Lee helped Clara off the bed and took her little hand in his own. "Pancakes it is. And you can make all the bubbles, because it's your first day of preschool." He wondered when she would grow up enough to realize that washing dishes wasn't really the treat he made it out to be.

He was still looking for a reason not to like the preschool as he drove the beater company truck he had borrowed from his construction company up to the quaint little house. Despite his efforts, and Clara's insanely early wake-up, they were still running late. It had started to snow, and he didn't want to push the truck too fast on the slushy streets. It had also, somehow, taken twenty minutes to get Clara into her winter coat and out the door, despite her eagerness to go.

He unstrapped Clara from her carseat and followed her with growing reluctance up the snowy steps. He wondered if he should have insisted she wear her winter boots, rather than the pink bear tennis shoes, but she scampered up and was pushing open the door before the snow had a chance to stick to her legs.

The door opened to a tiny Arctic entryway. Clara would have pushed further on, but Lee noticed the rack of coats and stopped her. "Here, honey, let's take off your coat."

She squirmed and fussed while he unzipped her and hung her coat on an empty hook.

It was warm, noisy chaos behind the second door. Children laughed and played at activity stations around the room, and someone was playing a cheerful song on a slightly tinny upright piano. As the musician, unseen, ended with a flourish, some of the children clapped in delight.

He wasn't ready. He'd been a fool to think he could do this–to leave Clara with some stranger for so many hours? He would just tell the old woman that he'd made a mistake, that Clara would be too anxious, that... he cast about in his mind for some excuse. That he'd forgotten her lunch? He settled a scowl on his face; that was often enough to send weak-willed people running, and maybe she wouldn't ask why he was withdrawing Clara from her class.

But Clara, not at all bothered by the noise, was trotting forward, her lunch clutched in one hand and the other pulling him reluctantly forward. "Her name is Miss Patricia," she said enthusiastically. "Aunt Bella said so."

Then "Miss Patricia" was bouncing out from behind the piano, and Lee's excuses died on his lips.

The gray bun and glasses he had imagined were nowhere to be seen. The tiny, ancient woman he had envisioned bore no resemblance to the blonde goddess who was smiling down at his daughter. She was tall and curvy, with big, brown eyes and straw-blonde hair loose to her shoulders. Energy radiated from her, and Lee felt like the floor had fallen away.

"You must be Clara," she was saying. Her voice sounded very far away–the sounds of the room had tunneled away in the shock of seeing her.

"I am," Clara said confidently. "I'm four. I brought my lunch."

"Let me show you where to put that," Miss Patricia said, and as she straightened, she met Lee's eyes.

Lee had never believed in soulmates; he thought the whole idea of a destined mate was ridiculous, made up for people who need comforting fiction to get through their lives. But the teacher's eyes, infinite pools of brown warmth, were the first place he had ever felt truly at home. The bear in him rumbled in delight.

"You must be Mr. Montgomery," she said, and her voice was as rich as her eyes, with the subtle Midwestern accent that he hadn't known he adored.

Lee realized she was holding out her hand, and had no idea how long it had been there. "Lee," he said swiftly, reaching out too fast to shake it. Touching her skin was like being struck by lightning, and he had to make himself let go after a handshake that was too long and trailed away into simply holding onto her. He had never wanted so badly to kiss a complete stranger.

"Lee," she said, with amusement. "It's nice to meet you."

Then Clara was slipping out of his other hand and following the golden woman away. She moved like a dancer, all grace and efficiency of motion. If she filled out her flowered country shirt nicely, she filled out her simple jeans even better, and Lee was mesmerized to watch her bend over to show Clara where to put her lunch. Down at their level, she suddenly became a magnet to the children, and was swiftly swarmed by small people demanding her attention.

More attractive than her curves and soft hair–which were enough by themselves to send Lee into a stupor of desire–was an air of gentle affection that glowed around her. Her sweet smile and careful handling of the childrens' attention was enchanting to watch. She knew just which ones needed a little playful redirection of their energy, and which ones needed a gentle nudge to boost their confidence. Her movements were never sharp or angry. Her attention flowed between them seamlessly, and the entire room was warmed by her simple presence.

Lee did not realize that he was standing there, staring stupidly, until Clara trotted back to him and pulled on his hand. "Papa, you're supposed to leave now."

Lee felt his cheeks heat unexpectedly– he couldn't remember the last time he had blushed–and knelt to give Clara a swift hug. "Have a fun day, cub," he told her, and then he turned and fled in a rush of confusion.

PATRICIA KNEW THAT the first day of preschool after any break–even just Christmas–was always as much about the parents as it was the children. Few of them were really ready to say goodbye, and they dealt poorly with the children who were clingy. But so far, only one child that morning needed any serious distraction, and she was enchanted with the class rabbit in short order.

Harriette Ambler, as expected, was the worst of the mothers, a perfect storm of condescending and demanding. Her son, Trevor, was a meek little angel, but to hear Harriette talk–right in front of the poor boy!–he was a perfect devil, and she clearly doubted that Patricia was up to the challenge for a second semester. She elbowed a little girl out of the way in order to get Patricia's attention, and detailed the contents of his lunch (which were also written on the outside of his lunch bag), and insisted that he was not to participate in rough play or, from the sounds of it, anything fun. Patricia managed to catch Trevor's eye while his mother was turned away, and rolled her eyes at him with an exaggerated shrug. She was rewarded with a shy half-smile, swiftly hidden as Harriette scolded him for slouching.

"I'm sure we'll manage, Harriette," Patricia assured her buoyantly. "We'll see you at two!" Then she was able to herd Trevor off to a painting station and walk away to the piano. Left without an audience, the infuriating woman finally left, and Patricia launched into a cheerful song to celebrate.

The last parent on Patricia's list and the only one that she didn't already know was Leland Montgomery. In some ways, he was exactly as she expected–and in some ways nothing at all as she'd envisioned.

His sister, Bella, had explained that he was a single father, and Patricia braced herself for a spoiled or neglected child and a harried father who couldn't even be bothered to arrange his own child's education. She was unsurprised that he was running late, and came out from around the piano braced for excuses and unpleasant conflict–he would either be the kind of single father who hated women for hurting him, or the overprotective sort who would never believe their child had flaws. Either way, being late would already put him on the defensive.

The first shock was his size. He made the schoolhouse feel small with his great bulk. He played football in high school, she guessed, with those fabulous shoulders. He probably worked construction now. A glance out of the window confirmed that guess– a battered company truck was parked in front of the school.

But he didn't look like a blue-collar worker, despite the worn plaid shirt and the big hands. He looked like a model playing at being a lumberjack, with fine cheekbones and piercing blue eyes. A mop of thick dark hair above glowering eyebrows looked as artful and deliberate as the stubble across his chiseled jaw. It was the kind of face and build that made Patricia's knees feel weak, and she had to focus on the daughter––or embarrass herself by drooling, or possibly fainting dramatically at his feet. Since she was far too large and awkward to look good fainting, Patricia was happy to exchange smiles with the little girl instead.

Clara was as adorable as only a four-year-old with curls could be. Her chubby-cheeked smile of trust and excitement was the whole reason that Patricia had become a teacher. Meeting her father's watchful gaze gave her whole new reasons for other things, and Patricia had to reach deep to find the calmness to say, "You must be Mr. Montgomery."

"Lee," he said shortly, with a scowl, and he reached out to give her hand a shake. The touch of his hand on her own was like jumping into a cool swimming hole on a sweltering day, all shock and relief and excitement at once. He had calluses that confirmed her guess about his occupation, big, strong, rough-fingered hands that made her own feel small and dainty. She forgot to let go until it had become awkward.

"Lee," she repeated like an idiot, savoring the simple syllable. "It's nice to meet you."

Fortunately, Clara broke her stupor with her childlike enthusiasm, and Patricia was able to peel herself away from the gorgeous man to show her across the room to where the child cubbies were so she could stow her lunch.

"It has my name!" Clara exclaimed in delight, and she could point out all the letters. "I have two As," the little girl assured her solemnly. "But they aren't together."

That drew the attention of a little boy named Aaron, who pointed out that his As were together, and then they were the center of a swarm of children who wanted to meet the new girl. Coming from such a small town, the rest all knew each other already.

"We just moved here from the city," Clara told them. "Our house is falling apart, but Daddy will make it like new."

That prompted questions about the city, and Amber begged Patricia to read the City Mouse book, and somewhere in the chaos Clara slipped away to see her father and shoo him out the door. Patricia didn't watch him go, but could feel his exit from the room as if he'd taken all of the light with him. She had never been so disappointed to see a parent leave and wished for a foolish moment that Clara had been more needy and given him reason to linger longer.

# Chapter Two

L ee had no intention of being late to pick up Clara.
It had been embarrassing enough to arrive late dropping her off, but more than that, he could not wait to see Patricia again. He caught himself rubbing the hand she had held throughout the day, and thinking about that laughter in her eyes and the way her mouth moved when she spoke. His bear grumbled impatiently inside, eager to be in her magnetic presence again as soon as possible.

His was the first vehicle parked in front of the old schoolhouse, and he had to make himself wait until the hands on his watch showed that he was only a few minutes early. Just as he unlatched the rusty door to the borrowed truck, another car drove up, and he paused so they could pull in beside him. The woman who exited the unreasonably shiny purple Chrysler had fluffy hair more suited for the 80s piled on top of her head, a cellphone in one hand and was wearing high heels that were utterly silly in the slushy snow. As Lee extricated himself carefully from the truck–she had parked foolishly close and slightly crooked–he must have growled a little, because he suddenly had all of her unwelcome attention.

Blue eyes widened, and her existing conversation miraculously became unimportant. The cellphone was being tucked into a designer purse as she met him at the front of their vehicles.

"Oh heavens," she said breathlessly. "I didn't leave you much room there, did I." Observing this somehow entailed squeezing right up next to him and leaning past him to examine the gap.

"Nope."

Lee hoped that the brief answer would suffice for conversation, but the woman clutched her hand to her chest as if she had committed some heinous offense. "I'm so sorry!" she said dramatically. "It's such a new car, you know. I'm just not sure where I am when I'm driving!"

Lee refrained from noting that she was clearly not sure where she was when she *wasn't* driving, and backed off a step to retain some personal space. "It's fine," he said shortly, hoping to get past her.

She seemed to think his acceptance was license for further conversation. "I'm Harriette," she introduced herself, holding out a hand to shake that Lee could only helplessly compare to Patricia's. It was a tiny, limp hand, with overdone nails, flawlessly smooth skin, and none of Patricia's warmth or strength. "You must be Mr..."

"Montgomery," Lee said shortly, deliberately not offering his first name.

Harriette paused a moment, expecting it, and finally moved on, not yet relinquishing his hand. "Mr. Montgomery," she savored. "It's *so* lovely to meet you! You've just moved in, then?"

Lee recovered his hand, and nodded. He was disappointed that his usual scowl was not having the usual effect.

"I work in real estate," Harriette explained without invitation. She looked thoughtful and then guessed, "You must have bought the old Lawson place!"

"Yes." Lee wondered if he could elbow past her without being rude, as another car pulled up, then another, disgorging a flurry of mothers who converged on their space. Harriette looked affronted, but managed to turn it to her advantage by introducing him to the gaggle of women as if she were in a privileged position of knowledge.

"This is Mr. Montgomery," she told them, as if they were long-time chums. "He's bought the old Lawson place."

"Oh, the old Lawson place," a brunette with a short bob said eagerly, pushing forward to hang on his handshake. The wedding ring on her hand didn't seem to deter her from all but drooling on him. "That's such a lovely *big* house. A shame they let it get so run down."

"I'll be restoring it," Lee felt conversationally obligated to say, and this prompted an interested murmur, with speculative looks at the battered company truck. He was beginning to regret his choice to put on nicer clothing to pick up Clara; his efforts to make a better impression with Patricia were having the unfortunate side effect of making him look monetarily desirable to the housewife brigade.

To his relief, the door to the farmhouse opened then and a herd of children padded in coats and boots and overseen by a watchful assistant that wasn't Patricia came scampering down to interrupt them. He was able to pick Clara out of the crowd and swing her into his arms. "I like preschool," she said cheerfully.

"What a charming little girl," Harriette gushed at him, entirely ignoring the little boy who had come up to hand her the craft they had created that day. "She's so adorable!"

"We got to paint, and there was music and there is a rabbit and Aaron has two As together in his name and we sang songs and I wrote my name on this for you!" Clara's monologue was a welcome excuse to ignore Harriette, which Lee cheerfully did. He considered the gauntlet of other women eyeing him speculatively between him and the schoolhouse, then decided that retreat was to be preferred to attempting to see Patricia. He brushed past the obnoxious little woman and went around the truck to tuck Clara into her carseat. He would catch Patricia another time.

His bear growled discontentedly at him as they drove away, leaving Harriette with a deep scowl in front of her shiny purple car.

# Chapter Three

PATRICIA GLANCED OUT the window just in time to see Lee's pickup pull away. A pang of disappointment hit her, but she quickly pushed it away. That gorgeous man probably didn't even remember her from their meeting that morning. She, on the other hand, felt like her entire world had shifted in some way.

"Patricia, you fool," she chided herself, picking up the litter of toys left out by the window. "Love at first sight only happens in fairy tales." She, on the other hand, was a grown woman, far too old for such nonsensical ideas. She was just a little lonely and had reacted unreasonably to a particularly handsome man with a wonderful handshake.

"Isn't he a *dish*," Andrea said as she came back in, echoing Patricia's thoughts. The last child had been attached to their parent and the final car was pulling out of the driveway. "And that didn't escape the attention of any of those vulture mothers."

Patricia chuckled. New single men in town were always the object of a lot of attention, from women both married and not, and Lee was the type to get a lot of interest; he seemed to be poor, but was plenty good-looking enough to make up for that.

She looked up from the basket of toys to find Andrea looking at her appraisingly. "What?"

"You like him!"

Sometimes Andrea's powers of observation were uncanny. Patricia had accused her of witchcraft in jest once or twice, but the longer she knew the small, vibrant woman, the more she began to wonder.

This was another case of her guess hitting close to home, and Patricia felt her cheeks heat. "I... er... he's very... we've only barely met!"

Andrea smiled smugly and tossed her sleek, dark hair knowingly. "And you're far too pragmatic to believe in love at first sight."

Patricia had to laugh at herself. "I am," she insisted. "I know better. Besides, he's the father of one of my students. How inappropriate would that be?"

"No more inappropriate than any of the married women throwing themselves at his feet in our parking lot," Andrea said with a roll of her eyes. "Promise me that if the opportunity presents itself, you won't chicken out."

"There won't be..."

"Promise!" The top of Andrea's head might barely hit Patricia's collarbone, but she was all fire and vinegar.

"I promise!" Patricia said meekly.

Andrea gave her a skeptical look, then accepted Patricia's word with a solemn nod. "I'll hold you to that."

Patricia knew that she would.

Later that evening, as she tied an apron around her waist at her second job as a waitress, Patricia tried to convince herself that it was a moot promise anyway.

It wasn't like they were going to have a lot of opportunities to interact outside of a strict teacher-and-father relationship. By the time Clara graduated from preschool, he would undoubtedly have been snagged by one of the many interested women in town; he was too handsome to go with a cold bed for any longer than he wanted, and what did she have to offer him other than that? Though Green Valley wasn't a wealthy town, there were certainly citizens with more means than she had. Harriette, for example, had made a respectable pile of money in real estate. The idea of Lee with Harriette set Patricia's teeth on edge, and she didn't think it was only because the odious woman had made most of that money selling family farms to developers who were planning to put up cheap condos. She was trying to buy the schoolhouse Patricia taught preschool in, and rumor had it that the horrid woman had just taken earnest money for a quaint landmark farm that she planned to have leveled to make a series of cheap, cookie-cutter houses–part of her self-announced plan to make Green Valley a bedroom community for the nearest city.

Patricia was still steaming over that idea and fantasizing ways she could buy out the schoolhouse herself as she made her rounds of the tables at Gran's Grits, the smaller of the two diners in town. The dinner rush, every one a familiar face, was a welcome distraction from her thoughts.

When she heard the bell at the door ring again, she automatically narrowed the possible customers down in her head; they were too far off the highway to attract many strangers. "Evening, Stan!" she called over her shoulder, and she was turning with a menu in hand even as she realized something was different. She knew what she would see before she actually did–was it his wild, clean smell? Or some hint of his strong step on the floor? She had to make herself not stare; Lee was somehow more handsome even than she had remembered, and once again, Clara saved her from making a fool of herself by giving her a safe place to look. Her hands knew to grab a second menu, and she was able to joke, "How nice of you to bring your father out to dinner, Clara," as she led them to a table tucked into the corner. Her hands only shook a little as she passed the menu to Lee.

"Papa can only cook pancakes," Clara explained candidly.

"Well, our special tonight is..." for a moment Patricia's mind blanked completely. 'Me on a platter, would probably be inappropriate,' she reminded herself. That wasn't what Andrea had meant about taking an opportunity that presented itself, anyway. "Chicken pot pie," she remembered just before the moment got awkward. "I recommend it."

"You're my teacher," Clara said, with her face crinkled thoughtfully as Patricia helped her clamber onto a booster seat.

"I work here, too." She gave Lee a wry look and joked, "Being a preschool teacher in a town this small for three days a week doesn't exactly cover the mortgage." She immediately wondered if it was inappropriately frank, aware of the discretely (and not-so discretely) curious looks they were getting from other tables, and vowed to be more professional. "Can I bring you some drinks?"

Lee glanced at the laminated menu. "Iced tea," he selected. "And milk for Clara."

Patricia escaped to the kitchen.

Fortunately, Old George, the order cook, was the large, quiet, non-judgmental type, and he didn't say anything about the fact that she splashed cold water on her hot face before she dispensed the drinks and headed back out to the dining room to take their order.

"Does the popeye have spinach?" Clara wanted to know when she delivered their drinks.

"Pot pie, Honey," Lee corrected.

"Popeye," Clara repeated carefully.

Patricia exchanged an amused look with Lee before she could stop herself, and only blushed a little before explaining to Clara, "No, no spinach. It's a pie crust with a cream sauce and pieces of carrot, peas, potatoes, and chunks of chicken. It has mashed potatoes on top!"

"They have hot dogs," Lee suggested, looking at the child's portion of the menu.

But Clara had been convinced. "I want popeye!" She handed Patricia her menu imperiously.

"Two orders of the special, on your fine recommendation," Lee agreed, and he gave Patricia a smile that made her insides melt.

She took the menus and retreated to put the order in and pick up a tray of plates for another table.

"Gina says Harriette says he bought the old Lawson place," Norman told her as she refilled his water and asked after his satisfaction with the meal. He could always be counted on for good gossip through his daughter. Patricia hadn't checked Lee's address in the parent database, but she gave a healthy amount of doubt to anything that came through Gina. Particularly if it came by way of Harriette.

At another table, old Mrs. Fredricks cackled and beckoned Patricia close so she could stage-whisper, "He's gorgeous, honey! If you don't give him your number, I will!" Patricia laughed at her, and gave her a hug around the shoulders because she was already leaning in.

LEE TRIED HARD NOT to watch Patricia waltz around the little diner too obviously, but it was a small room, and she filled it with her golden presence. The tenderness and warmth he had witnessed with the preschool children apparently extended to people taller than three feet, and he found himself growing envious of her easy affection.

He had never been grateful for how slow Clara usually ate before, but this time, he could have kissed her for dawdling. Half a plate of pot pie became the occupation of an hour, then two. A spilled half-glass of milk took up another several minutes, and Lee considered spilling his own drink in order to watch Patricia kneel to clean up the mess with her forgiving laugh again.

The other diners gradually trickled out, until they were the only occupants of the cheerful room.

"I've never had so many dessert orders," Patricia told him, as she brought him the bill with two cello-wrapped mints. "Everyone in town wants to stay to see the most interesting little girl," she teased Clara, but she gave Lee a little half-glance that suggested it wasn't Clara who was really getting all the attention. Her cheeks colored, and she added professionally, "I'll be your cashier when you're ready to go."

Lee was used to women trying to flatter Clara to get his own attention, and he was used to them falling all over him even without her. Patricia, on the other hand, gave every indication of being attracted to him, but offered no hint of pursuit. She flirted more with the last old man to leave than she did with him, and her attention to Clara seemed completely genuine. It made the bear in him want to chase her more than ever, but he was absurdly uncertain how to do that. This was a problem he'd never encountered.

So he just watched her clear tables as he got Clara into her coat and boots, and after agonizing over the tip for a moment—would too much seem like he was trying to buy her?—he left her exactly a 15% tip on the credit card receipt, calculated to the penny.

At the door, he paused. "Thank you," he said.

Clara echoed him as he struggled to find something to add. "Thank you, Miss Patricia!"

"You're very welcome," Patricia called back. "I'll see you tomorrow!"

Then she was bustling away with their bill and the last glass, sparing him any conversation at all.

His bear wanted to chase her quite literally, but he reined in the beast and took Clara by the hand. He could be patient. He would have to be patient.

# Chapter Four

THE CHEERFUL CHIME of the door alarm got Patricia's heart racing every time it sounded, even though she knew it was more likely to be one of their familiar regulars, and looking around so quickly was only giving herself whiplash. She brought extra napkins to Norman, whose hands shook more than he liked to admit these days, and gathered the dirty dishes off of Mrs Fredricks' table, shaking her head at her foolishness.

She forced herself not to look when the bell rang again as she was taking Stan's order, faced away from the door, but she couldn't keep the ridiculous hope from rising in her throat.

Turning to discover Lee standing at the entry with Clara's mittened hand in his own made her blush, and smile too broadly, and then nearly sneeze trying to get her face back under some kind of control.

"Good evening," she sang too loudly, bringing them menus and gesturing to the same table they had sat at before. "I'll be right back to tell you our specials for this evening."

She fled to the kitchen, where Old George cracked a rare smile at her when she couldn't remember what Stan had ordered.

"He came in last night, too," the cook rumbled. "Looked disappointed you weren't here."

"He's a single guy who can't cook," Patricia explained. "There aren't that many choices in town!"

George shrugged and started making Stan's usual, sending Patricia back out with a plate to deliver.

Patricia got it to the destination without problem, trying not to turn herself too obviously so that she could watch Lee's table out of the corner of her eye. She took a deep breath, then brought an iced tea and a milk to Lee's table. "We've got a chipped beef with toast tonight," she said. "It's one of George's specialties."

Lee looked bemusedly at the iced tea.

"I, ah, should have asked if you wanted that again," Patricia said, suddenly realizing that it had been presumptuous of her.

"Oh, I do!" Lee said quickly. "It's good tea. Very lemony. Not too sweet."

"There's sugar, if you want it sweeter," Patricia said, pointing out the very obvious sugar caddy at the far edge of the table, then felt ridiculous, because he'd just said that it wasn't too sweet.

"Right," Lee said.

Clara, who had been stacking her coat and mittens in the empty chair beside her, chose that beautiful moment to say, "I could add sugar to my milk!" She reached eagerly for the tin.

Lee snagged the sugar caddy and brought it out of her easy reach. "I don't think so, kitten. Milk doesn't need sugar."

"Aaron's mom says you need sugar," Clara said candidly.

Lee and Patricia both choked on their laughter, and couldn't quite meet each other's eyes.

Patricia cleared her throat, casting about for a safe topic. "We do have fresh brownies made, for dessert."

"If you eat your dinner," Lee added quickly, as Clara bounced at the idea.

"A hot dog!" Clara declared, handing the menu to Patricia. "I'll eat the whole thing!"

"I'll take the special, and hold us two brownies," Lee said, and then he did meet Patricia's eyes.

It was like basking in sunlight; his gorgeous blue eyes were something she could drown in, if she let herself. *Don't flirt, don't flirt,* Patricia told herself ferociously, though she wasn't able to keep herself from blushing. She had seen how the preschool moms pounced on him, two days in a row now, and how coldly he had reacted. "Sounds great!" she said with a big, friendly smile that didn't invite anything more, and she didn't come back to the table until she had their plates ready.

Lee tried several times to strike up conversation, to Patricia's surprise. She answered his questions about Green Valley as simply as she could and found other tasks to pursue, reminding herself fiercely that she shouldn't attempt to draw him out, trying to balance a light friendly air with her ridiculous desire to throw herself down in his lap and beg him to kiss her.

Gran's Grits closed early, specializing in breakfast and lunch with dinner as an afterthought, so Lee and Clara were once again the last customers. Clara held true to her promise to eat the whole hot dog, but slowed drastically halfway through the big brownie. The ice cream it had been served with melted into a puddle, but she continued to nibble at it as Patricia cleared away Lee's dessert plate and she brought him the copy of his receipt with his credit card.

Their hands touched as he took it, and Patricia froze. He didn't move his fingers, and when Patricia dared to lift her gaze to his face, he was looking at her with a curious, intense look. She was keenly aware of where their skin was just touching, and it wasn't until she realized that she was trembling a little that she could let go of the tray with the copy of the bill. He wasn't expecting her sudden movement, and it fell a few inches to table with a clatter that startled Clara, who had been starting to doze off in that glaze-eyed way that children could manage while still sitting upright.

"I'm tired," the little girl said plaintively, and the moment was shattered.

Lee's attention was all for Clara again, and Patricia fled to the kitchen while they bundled up in their coats and left.

# Chapter Five

JUST AS LEE TURNED off the power sander, the sound of the doorbell jarred him out of his working reverie. "Coming!" he hollered, navigating the maze of sawhorses and power tools to get to the big receiving room.

The house was a chaos of moving boxes and construction sites. Fully half of the house was still being refinished, with painter's tape on all the trim and plastic taped over the old fireplaces. Only Clara's bedroom and his own had been fully finished, as well as the bathrooms for both of them, and the kitchen downstairs, which had been gutted and combined with servant's quarters to become one big open, airy space with a breakfast nook. The outside looked worse, with the siding power-washed but not repainted before the winter had settled in. Two of the windows in the unfinished wing were boarded up. The roof was due for a full replacement, but had been temporarily patched and tarped in places, giving the house a look of utter disrepute.

Lee's frustration at being interrupted in his work turned to fear when he flung open the door and saw Patricia standing on the porch, the limp form of Clara over one shoulder, draped in a puffy orange and blue down coat dusted with snow. Behind her, big, fat flakes of snow were blanketing the yard and obscuring the view of the valley.

"Clara," Lee said, fighting past the paralyzing fear. "Clara?"

"She's fine," Patricia said swiftly, and Clara stirred and mumbled, putting her arms more firmly around her teacher's neck. "She just fell asleep on the way over."

"It's not time to pick her up yet," Lee said lamely, checking his watch to confirm. His heart rate eased only slightly at the relief of his daughter's safety; being this close to Patricia made him feel all undone and filled with need. His bear growled inappropriate suggestions at him.

"It's snowing like the apocalypse," Patricia explained, carrying Clara in gently. When Lee went to take her, trying not to be distracted by the delicious warm scent of snow melting in Patricia's hair, Clara buried her head further into Patricia's shoulder and protested wordlessly. "We canceled the last half of school today. I tried to call, but it went straight to voicemail. The roads were getting so bad, I wanted to get her home while we could still make it."

Lee remembered the blinking red battery symbol on the phone when he'd hung up with his sister Bella. He hadn't put it back on the charger. "We haven't gotten a landline yet," he said apologetically.

"You, ah, seem to have a bit of a work in progress here," Patricia said diplomatically.

"Clara's room is finished," he said defensively.

When another attempt to remove Clara from Patricia's shoulder met sleepy protest, he said, "Bring her this way," just as Patricia said, "Maybe I should put her into bed..."

The grand front steps had not been refinished yet, but the upper hall had been, and Lee was gratified when Patricia stepped into Clara's room and said with a little gasp, "Oh!"

Lee had spared no expense on the room, and had let Clara take a role in the decoration. She had picked a mermaid theme, one that Lee wholeheartedly approved of. The walls were teal blue and white, with decals of tropical fish, coral, and sunken treasure. The bed had a shell-shaped headboard, and a shimmery bedspread of blue. A windowseat as broad as her bed was cluttered with seashell pillows and an enormous knitted red squid. Short bookshelves lined one wall, filled with books and coloring books and bins of crayons and blocks. There was a dollhouse in one corner, and a riding-size excavator and dumptruck, but the current feature of the room was a battered moving box with a door and several windows cut out. Childish artwork adorned every wall and part of the roof, and a small table (another moving box) was inside and spread out for tea with a lace tablecloth. Across the room, white doors were open to show a walk-in closet and a glimpse at a private bath.

Patricia took her armful to the bed as Lee drew the curtains shut, and she peeled off Clara's boots and laid her down. Lee, watching her helplessly, could only marvel at how perfect and wonderful it was to watch her draw the blankets up over his daughter, smoothing the comforter up around her shoulders as Clara gave a contented sigh and snuggled in. He flipped the light switch, and Patricia padded her way out by the light from a muted blue nightlight.

The click of Clara's door closing seemed to be a changing point, and if Lee had been painfully aware of her nearness in any other way, he was suddenly keenly aware of her as only a woman now–his woman. His soulmate. They were alone, in his house, and she was standing close enough that he could smell the delicate scent of her shampoo. His erection was making his utilitarian jeans uncomfortable, and he had to wrestle back the bear who was singing in his head that she was his, and to take her now.

*If I make a move now, she'll run*, he thought. *She needs a... subtle touch.* "I could... ah... show you the rest of the house," he offered.

Patricia looked up at him and bit her lip, her eyes shy but steady. "You could show me your bedroom," she said in a rush.

It was all the invitation Lee needed; his heart filled with triumph. He enfolded her into his arms and kissed her.

# Chapter Six

IF PATRICIA COULD BRING herself to be jealous of a four-year-old girl, she might have been jealous of Clara. Her bedroom was like walking into a fairy tale fantasy, and filled with things that even grown-up Patricia would have enjoyed playing with. Four-year-old Patricia would have had raptures.

Twenty-six-year-old Patricia was having raptures at the closeness of Lee, instead. He was wearing only a tight t-shirt that hid nothing of his amazing physique, and he smelled like sawdust and sweat and manliness that was deeply distracting. Patricia tucked Clara in and retreated from the bedroom, Andrea's admonition ringing in her mind.

This was an opportunity. This was *the* opportunity. There would never be another opportunity so opportune.

Was she reading his signals wrong? Was he really attracted to her? She thought she caught his gaze lingering, wondered if he didn't smile at her just a touch more than the conversations they had deserved, but maybe she was misreading the situations.

The door to Clara's room shut with a tiny click, and they paused together. "I could... ah... show you the rest of the house?"

The way he offered, so tentatively and hopefully, gave Patricia the rest of the courage she needed. She made herself hold his gaze and brazenly offered, "You could show me your bedroom."

She had a split second to wonder at her own forwardness, then he was kissing her, pressing against the length of her, his embrace like a bear's as his mouth found her own.

Her doubts vanished with his kiss–he kissed her with his whole body and being, and Patricia felt like she was being swept away in a river of passion. His erection was hard against her through the fabric of his jeans. She clutched at his shoulders helplessly, tipping her head to take as much of his kiss as she could. They collided with the wall of the hallway, and broke apart, shushing each other and giggling.

"The bedroom," Lee said breathlessly. "This way..."

They kissed and grabbed the entire length of the unadorned hall, plucking at each other's clothing as they went and running into the walls twice more before Lee opened the door to his own bedroom and they fell inside.

His hands were big and callused, but gentle and nimble, and Patricia's shirt was off before they'd made it halfway to the bed. She had his belt unfastened and was working on his jeans by the time they'd made it to the wide bed, and they paused a moment together, gasping for breath. Lee's gaze could only be classified as 'appreciative,' and Patricia didn't even try not to stare back. If anything, the tight t-shirt had only been a tease, and the physique beneath was even more delicious. His shoulders were thick with muscles, and his core rippled with abs. And as amazing and gorgeous as his body was, it was his face that continued to draw her back. He was beautiful, and his eyes were adoring in a way that made Patricia weak and wet.

"I'm not usually like this," she said, swallowing. She'd made her last boyfriend wait three weeks of dating before she'd taken off her shirt. What was it about this man that made her so crazy?

"I'm not, either," Lee said, and just the sound of his husky voice made her knees tremble.

Then he leaned in and kissed her, and it was a different kiss than the first–less passionate, but more controlled, deeper, and more meaningful. Patricia lost herself entirely in it, putting her arms around his neck and letting him lay her back down onto the silky bedspread.

He released his kiss, only to move it to her neck, which left her writhing in helpless excitement, and resumed undressing her. He unclipped her bra first, slipping it off her with reverence, and then slid a finger into the waistband of her jeans as he kissed the breasts he revealed, toying with her a moment before unbuttoning and slowly– so slowly!–unzipping her jeans. Patricia whimpered and clutched at his thick hair and broad shoulders. She wanted to beg him to hurry, but was enjoying the build-up too entirely to truly protest.

He shimmied her out of her jeans with no effort, stroking her thighs and kissing her tummy as he did so. Patricia couldn't help but squirm and screw her eyes shut to try to stem the overwhelming cascade of sensation. She must be wet right through her simple cotton panties–there was no way he couldn't notice how excited she was.

Then he paused, and her eyes flew open as he shifted on the bed. He was suddenly not moving slowly at all, but tearing off his own jeans, and releasing the huge erection she had felt earlier. She was glad that her eyes were open for the reveal– he was magnificent!–but also rather alarmed. It didn't look geometrically possible for it to fit within her. Then he was tearing her panties off and growling like an animal, the weight of him deflecting the bed around her as he straddled her, and she wanted nothing more than to take the entire thing right then.

"Please," she murmured, and he was burying himself into her with one long, slow thrust, filling her with his length and heat.

PATRICIA ARCHED UP into his advance, gasping and clawing and begging in a way that lit Lee on fire. His need for her was deep and wild, but he concentrated on her pleasure first, and was rewarded by her blistering orgasm and moan of delight within a few careful thrusts. Her cry was passionate and she tensed beautifully before relaxing in the wake of her release. He kissed her neck and shoulders, pinning her under him on the bed, but had to slow himself to an agonizingly slow speed, or risk cutting off their fun too soon with his mounting need.

She kissed him back, then rolled until she was straddling him, her luscious breasts swinging in rhythm as she took him deep inside her.

She was glorious, riding above him, matching his leisurely speed until he had wound himself into a frenzy. "If you don't stop, I'm going to–"

She only sped up, the vixen, and clutched at his shoulders as she achieved another moaning, arching orgasm, and her pleasure was the inescapable catalyst of his own sexual climax.

He flung his arms out and clutched at the blankets on either side as she rode him wildly and they both came with abandon.

Patricia collapsed atop him, and Lee continued to thrust slowly in the afterglow of his pleasure until the last ripple of the orgasm was finally played out.

"Oomph," she said finally, voice husky near her ear. "I'm too heavy to lay on you like this."

In response, Lee wrapped his arms around her and held her close. He loved the feel of her curves against him, the silky touch of her skin along the whole length of his body, and wasn't willing to let her go quite yet. She didn't struggle, only gave a blissed-out sigh and snuggled closer.

"I'm not usually like this," she said, as she had earlier, and Lee chuckled.

"I'm not, either," he agreed.

But then, it wasn't every day that he made love to his soul-mate, either. He rolled over so that they were side-by-side on the bedspread, and he could look directly into her face.

"This... is terribly unprofessional of me," she confessed.

"Are you sorry?" he had to ask.

Her face took on an impish expression. "Not in the slightest."

He had to cup her face in his hand and kiss her again, to see if he could taste the laughter on her lips. She kissed back with all of her earlier passion, and Lee knew that he could be ready for her again in short order. She was the most perfect armful that he had ever held, and there was a feeling of loss when she slipped away from him and went rummaging for her clothing.

"The bathroom is through that door," he indicated, and he sat up in the bed just to appreciate her graceful pad across the plush carpet.

Then he flopped back across the bed. He had to tell her. He had to explain that she was the one for him–the only one. She was his everything, for all that they'd only known each other a few short months, and he wasn't willing to let her get away.

He'd have to tell her about being a bear.

That was where he tripped up. It was an impossible conversation to have.

"I'm a bear shifter," he imagined himself saying. "I can turn into a grizzly bear." She would laugh and not believe him. Would he have to shift, and prove it? Would she react with terror and flee him? Faint on the spot? He just couldn't imagine Patricia fainting. Shooting him, maybe–she looked like the kind of farmgirl who had handled a gun before.

He'd never told anyone before–not even Clara's mother. Guilt and confusion chilled him, and he found himself rising and going to one of the unpacked moving boxes. A pile of framed photographs were stacked near the top–photos of Angela, and Clara as a baby. He hadn't been able to bring himself to hang them yet, using the state of the rest of the house as some kind of excuse for not hanging things here in the bedroom yet. He tried to tell himself he liked the austere bareness of the off-white walls with the pearly-gray carpet.

Mostly, he couldn't bear to have Angela looking at him from those walls.

This was a new house, a new start. He wanted this to be his house with Patricia, though he hadn't known that until he met her. But wasn't it unfair to Angela's memory to cut her out?

Wasn't it cruel to Clara to have her mother excluded from their family walls? It felt like a terrible disservice to his brief years of marriage, and even now, years later, he had difficulty separating his grief and his guilt from his memories of joy.

# Chapter Seven

PATRICIA GAVE A LITTLE gasp as she went through the empty walk-in closet to the master bath. From the little hallway, it opened up into an oasis of marble and chrome. The shower door was pristine, clear glass, and there were two showerheads, one from each side. Beside it was a jetted bathtub in the corner, big enough for several people at once. A counter with two sinks ran the length of the room just opposite, and the toilet was tucked around a discrete corner. Big windows opened out over a winter wonderland of trees and snow-covered lawn.

She turned on the water and watched the windows fog with steam. It was enchanted, magical, like making love to Lee had been.

And just as impermanent.

She would shower and get dressed, then go home and then they would pretend this had never happened. It was the best possible outcome.

She showered swiftly, though she wanted to savor the delicious heat and roomy shower. Lee apparently had only a single kind of shampoo/body wash, and Patricia had no regrets lathering herself in the manly scent.

She dressed as efficiently as she had washed, but left her socks off rather than try to pull them on over her wet feet. She was drying her hair with one of the big plush towels (there was no sign of a hair-dryer and Patricia was loathe to snoop through his drawers) as she walked back to the bedroom and she had to pause in the doorway with her breath caught in her throat.

Lee was sitting at the edge of the bed looking away, his big shoulders bowed. There was a framed photograph in his hands. Patricia couldn't see the subject of the photograph, but she could guess: Clara's mother. Had she been the first since...?

The scene felt painfully intimate, and Patricia wrestled with her desire to go immediately comfort Lee, and the sad understanding that she could not, and that she was simply not part of Lee's intimate sphere. She wanted to be, she realized keenly. It wasn't just that she was irresistibly attracted to this man; she would have admired him with half the looks just for his handling of Clara, and every time they spoke, she found something new to like in him. She wanted him on levels that she'd never experienced before, and always thought she never would. Her friends would talk about true love and settling down, but she had never wanted to, until Lee.

Now, unexpectedly, she wanted nothing more.

She chewed on her lower lip, then crept backwards several steps. If she couldn't be his everything, she could be the best for him that she could at least, and that meant letting him keep his dignity. She started humming, and was whistling by the time she came back into the doorway so that he had a chance to toss the photograph back into the box and sit up straight.

"What a shower," she gushed, as if she hadn't witnessed a thing. "That whole bathroom is a work of art. You must have spent a fortune on that room alone!"

He looked uncomfortable–Patricia couldn't decide if it was because he knew he'd been caught in his moment of vulnerability, or because she was talking about money again like an idiot.

She clamped her mouth around her desire to babble moronically and tried to simply appreciate the view. That wasn't too hard–he was lounging in unselfconscious nudity, and his muscles were ripples of masculinity under a layer of perfect, barely-tanned skin. She was sorely tempted to tear off her clothing and go diving back into that bed again.

"I should... ah..." Not undress and throw myself at him again... "Be leaving. Before the snow gets too deep to get home."

Lee was standing up now, and he was as impressive upright as he was reclining across the sheets. "I fear you are too late for that," he said apologetically, with a gesture towards the window.

The snow was coming down in a soft curtain now, too thick to see even to where the driveway curved. Patricia's car was already blanketed in nearly a foot of snow. "Oh gosh, it's pretty," she said. "Like a dream." Lee was close behind her, smelling like sex and forest and wildness, and he was part of the whole crazy dream.

He put his hands on her shoulders–big hands, strong hands, *sexy* hands, and said in a voice like chocolate, "I suspect you are stuck here for a little while, at least."

"Papa! Papa!"

Clara's voice from down the hall had them scrambling apart. Lee dressed himself so swiftly that Patricia was still trying to figure out what to do with her own hands when he was back in his clothing and striding out the door.

"Miss Patricia brought me home!" Clara said enthusiastically when they met in the hallway, her blonde curls rumpled from her nap. "And it's snowing white! It never snowed white at home!"

Patricia chuckled. "It didn't snow *white*?"

"Only gray! Everything was dirty!" Clara seemed utterly nonplussed to find that her teacher was still there, hair still damp from a shower, and took her hand with authority. "Can I need a snack and go play in the white snow?"

"I think that's a remarkably good idea," Lee agreed. "Let's go show Miss Patricia the kitchen."

# Chapter Eight

LEE AND PATRICIA WALKED with Clara between them down the stairs and back to the sprawling kitchen. He couldn't keep himself from glancing over, watching the profile of her smiling face as she entertained Clara's endless prattle.

His mate.

There was bone-deep contentment just being close to her, knowing that she was his. All of his earlier concerns and worries were swept away in the simple peace of her presence.

Her delight in the kitchen was almost (but not quite!) as rewarding as her delight in his body had been. Clara gave her a gabby tour, opening every cabinet in her reach and pointing out all of the others.

"The blender is there, I'm not allowed to touch it and it's very loud. That's a mixer! I'm allowed to play with the plastic things in here."

Patricia was a rapt audience. "Oh, that's lovely! What a beautiful plate! Such soft towels!"

She said more seriously to Lee, "This kitchen is a cook's fantasy, Mr. Montgomery. If I had designed my dream kitchen straight from scratch, it could not have been more perfect." She actually squealed a little when she saw the heavy-duty mixer.

"I've never used it, but I asked our cook to make a list of everything he wanted in a kitchen," he explained, half-apologetically as he stacked up a few dirty dishes from lunch that he hadn't washed yet.

"Your cook had excellent taste," Patricia said, with delight.

"In all things but choosing to stay in the city," Lee agreed. "We'll have a housekeeper in a few weeks, I hope," he added apologetically, aware of his dirty lunch dishes and the sawdust footprints he had tracked into the kitchen.

Clara got herself a plate with a pile of peanut butter and an apple, which Patricia cut into careful wedges for her, exclaiming over the high-quality chef's knife. Clara settled herself in the booster cushion at the kitchen table.

"There is a formal dining room," Lee explained. "But we're still waiting for the dining set to be delivered."

When Clara had finished eating, graciously sharing her last two slices with Lee and Patricia, she insisted on showing Patricia the rest of the house.

Their last stop was after a full circle back to the dining room. "We'll eat here when we have a table," Clara explained, tugging Patricia through the doorway. Lee followed them. "This is my favorite room! Except for my own room. And Papa's room. And the kitchen."

"I can see why," Patricia said without sounding patronizing. It was a big, empty room with a hardwood floor. The only furniture was a built-in sidebar and a single padded bench that had been put there temporarily. "It's such a lovely, big room. It's perfect for dancing! I bet you dance here all the time."

Cornflower eyes blinked up at her. "I don't know how to dance."

"Don't know how to dance?" Patricia looked genuinely alarmed at the idea. "How can you not know how to dance?"

"I never took classes for it." Clara looked at Lee for guidance.

Patricia's laugh was reassuring. "You don't need classes, sweetheart! You just dance from inside! Everyone is born knowing how to dance!" She held out her hand to Clara. "Come dance with me!"

Clara hung back. "There isn't any music," she said, but she looked hopeful, and interested. It gave Lee a pang of guilt. Perhaps he should have insisted on lessons earlier.

Patricia pulled her phone out of her pocket, opened the music program, and put it on the sideboard. The music was terribly tinny, and it sounded like an old-time radio. She offered a hand to Clara.

This time, Clara took Patricia's hand, and a slow smile bloomed on her face. "Can Papa dance, too?"

"Of course he can!" Patricia met Lee's eyes with dancing mischief and held out her other hand to him.

"Oh, no, I..."

Patricia was already pulling Lee into the middle of the room.

"No, really, I can't..."

"It isn't rocket science," Patricia promised laughingly. "You just move around to the beat!"

Clara was willing to do what he was willing to do, so Lee followed Patricia's lead obediently, suspecting at once that she was making things more ridiculous than they needed to be. They bounced and wiggled and twisted their hips–shy at first and awkward, then looser and more joyous to match Patricia as she teased and encouraged them.

They did silly moves–the twist and the moonwalk–and Patricia showed Clara the first two ballet positions to a pop version of the nutcracker.

The phone went to a slow ballad, and Patricia showed Clara how to waltz with her little bare feet on Patricia's bare feet.

Delighted, Clara danced a round of the room with Lee in the same fashion, and then gave him over to Patricia expectantly.

Lee took one hand and put his other at her waiting waist, suddenly feeling awkward. "I really don't dance," he protested, despite their antics of moments ago.

"Not on my feet, you don't," Patricia laughed at him. Her cheeks were bright with exertion, and her hair was drying from her shower in soft, golden waves around her face.

She led him patiently around the room, praising his rhythm, and correcting his form. He stumbled over her feet several times, but she only laughed off his apologies. He grew braver as they danced, holding her closer and finding it easier to sway to the beat. The smell of her, and the warmth of her close against him filled him with contentment and joy.

He could have continued to hold onto Patricia much longer, but Clara wanted another turn balanced on his feet, and he carefully cavorted her around the room again, feeling more effortless about it with every bar of music.

Finally, Lee and Patricia collapsed together on the bench by the wall. The intimacy and energy of the dancing made it natural to sit leaning close together, and he wove his hand into hers without thinking about it. Clara continued to jump and spin in giddy delight.

"Never danced!" Patricia said, shaking her head in astonishment. "You're a natural," she praised.

"I want to dance for always," Clara said, pure joy in every line of her body.

Lee didn't realize he was scowling or squeezing Patricia's hand too tightly until he caught her quizzical look, but he wasn't prepared to explain why the simple statement hit him so hard.

"It's almost time for dinner," he deflected.

"Can Miss Patricia stay for dinner?" Clara stopped dancing and asked, her voice already taking on a whine in preparation for a fight.

"Miss Patricia is stuck here for the night, sweetie," Lee explained. "There's too much snow outside for her to drive home." He gestured at the window, where the evening gloom had a strange snowy brightness.

Clara squealed in absolute delight, flinging herself into Patricia's lap for a big hug and then leaning across her for a bonus hug from Lee. "She can stay in Aunt Bella's room," she suggested happily, sprawled bonelessly across their laps with the ease of a small child.

"Yes, of course," Lee and Patricia said in unison, just a little too fast. They glanced at each other and Lee felt a smile tug at the corner of his mouth. Her answering smile was a delicious promise of things to come.

Lee had never been so grateful to the weather.

"Let me cook for you?" Patricia offered, untangling her fingers from Lee's. "As a thank you for your... hospitality." She blushed beautifully.

# Chapter Nine

PATRICIA HAD NOT EXAGGERATED her appreciation for Lee's kitchen. Everything was thoughtfully laid out on broad counters. A whole series of beautiful knives, perfectly sharpened, were just out of easy child's reach, and she had her choice of gorgeous hardwood cutting boards.

She found a full set of high-end spices, and was not surprised that none of them except the garlic had been unsealed. The refrigerator revealed a gallon of milk and a wealth of condiments, but few other perishables. A few plastic take-out containers were stacked in one corner. An investigation of the pantry discovered a selection of canned vegetables, pastas, and staples. Patricia suspected by their perfect organization that they had not been touched. An untidy row of macaroni and cheese boxes suggested what they usually ate.

After puzzling over the ingredients for a while, Patricia put together a spaghetti sauce from a can of tomatoes, some frozen breakfast sausages, and a sad forgotten bell pepper from the bottom of the crisper. Clara danced around her feet while she cooked, asking to see and smell everything, and Lee sat at the table, watching her move around the kitchen with unsettling–but strangely comfortable–attention. She boiled the noodles, and toasted garlic toast under the broiler.

He set the table, with Clara's help, and when she set the plates in front of them, they both gushed their pleasure and delight. She sat at the third space at the table, and they merrily shared the meal together.

"I had no idea there was anything so... edible that could be made from these ingredients," Lee confessed, mopping the last of his sauce from the plate. "I'm not sure how to thank you."

Patricia loved how relaxed his face was. There was no trace of the scowl that seemed to be his usual default expression with other people, only warm smiles and dancing blue eyes. "Maybe tomorrow you can make me pancakes," she suggested. She smiled at Clara. "I've heard so much about them."

"It's a deal," Lee said.

Sharing in Clara's night time routine seemed perfectly natural. The little girl had her own mermaid-themed bathroom, with a shell-shaped tub just her size. After a bath heaped with bubbles, she toweled herself off and insisted that it was Miss Patricia who helped her into her fuzzy-footed pajamas.

"I wish I had footy-pajamas with kitties on them," Patricia said with only mostly-mock envy.

"What do you sleep in?" Clara asked innocently.

Patricia had to bite her lip and studiously not look at Lee. She couldn't exactly admit she liked to sleep naked.

Lee didn't help matters. "Good question, Sweetie," he said, straight-faced. Humor danced in his eyes. "What DO you sleep in, Miss Patricia?"

Patricia was beginning to suspect that there was pure mischief behind the scowl that Lee had cultivated. Well, two could play that game. "Not a stitch," she admitted brazenly, looking right at him. "I figure if I can't wear fuzzy-footed kitty-cats, why wear anything?"

Clara accepted the idea without question, but Patricia took great glee in watching the tips of Lee's ears turn pink.

It was Lee that tucked Clara into bed, and Patricia retreated to the hall so they could read their favorite book together and share a quiet, murmured conversation before Lee pulled the covers up to her chin, kissed her on the brow, and turned off her bedside light.

He shut her door with a careful click, and Patricia's heart melted at the tender look on his face. He loved that little girl more than the moon. The look didn't fade as he held Patricia's gaze, and the moment grew more tense.

Patricia found herself blushing. "This is... er... familiar. Didn't we do this just this afternoon?"

"I hope we'll do this many more times," Lee said, voice husky as he gathered her into his arms and kissed her.

Patricia's heart leapt in her chest at the idea. He wanted to see her again! This wasn't a one-freak-snowstorm affair, but maybe something more... She caught herself short at the idea. Just because he wanted to continue their relationship didn't indicate he meant that relationship as more than just a comfort of the body. She was probably just... convenient.

"I think you should get into what you sleep in, too," Lee suggested, and his kiss slipped down to her neck. Patricia stopped thinking about pesky relationship thoughts and let him lead her down the hallway to his bedroom.

"Won't I be sleeping in Aunt Bella's room?" she suggested mischievously, pausing at his door.

Lee drew back from kissing her and scowled in a now-familiar way. "Do you *want* to sleep in Bella's room?"

Patricia wrapped her arms around his neck. "Not in the slightest," she laughed at him.

To her astonishment, he picked her up, without the slightest hint of effort, and carried her to his waiting bed, nudging the door shut behind him with one foot.

He undressed her efficiently, but paused at each layer of clothing. "Is this what you sleep in?" he would ask.

Patricia pretended to consider it. "A little bit less," she encouraged.

He kissed her, wherever was closest, and peeled off another layer. Patricia couldn't decide if she was glad for the Midwest winter encouraging her to wear so many layers, or if she cursed it.

But the time he got to her underwear, she was quivering with anticipation and desire. He slid a finger into the waistband. "Is this what you sleep in?" he asked, mouth close to her stomach.

"A little bit less," Patricia said breathlessly.

He drew off the simple white underwear–she was too distracted to wish she had dressed with more care that morning, but how could she have anticipated this kind of a snow day!–and kissed her mound, tongue flickering inside her and making her arch up in an agony of desire and need.

"Oh, *Lee*," she said, and she loved the way his simple name tasted in her mouth almost as much as she loved the way he felt teasing her with his tongue.

He coaxed a long, delicious orgasm from her with his lapping thrusts, and when she could see straight again, Patricia tipped up on her elbows and demanded, "And what do you plan on sleeping in, Mr. Montgomery?"

Lee pulled his shirt off with one deft move. "I like your choice of attire," he said with a slow, sexy smile.

Patricia helped him pull off his pants and free the erection that she'd been dying to see again. She wrapped bold fingers around it, and delighted in the involuntary gasp that he gave. She stroked it gently, and explored it with fingertips, observing which motions set his jaw to clenching, curious to see how much teasing he could take.

He growled at her, finally, and tilted her back onto the waiting bed with a slow, tender pressure.

Patricia lifted her hips to meet him, and he slipped into her waiting entrance, filling her slowly, irresistibly, until she cried out and clawed at the blankets in an agony of delight.

He brought her to orgasm, then slowed as the ripples of pleasure ebbed away, thrusting gently and smiling in self-satisfaction as she recovered. She had to laugh at his expression, then pulled him down and tumbled sideways with him until she was on top and could take control of the situation herself. There was so much strength in him, that he had to let her do it, and she was equal parts delighted by this and challenged by it.

She straddled him with authority, riding him enthusiastically, but careful not to let him get too close to release. He held her waist, explored her swinging breasts, and even reached up to cradle her face as they pulsed together. Patricia forgot her plan to keep him thirsting for her, and lost herself in the flames of passion, cresting to another orgasm just as he sped up and took his own final pleasure, hot seed erupting in her.

They lay together, gasping for breath and balance, for a long, delicious moment. He continued to caress her, bringing the lovemaking to a beautiful trailing end that Patricia had never known could be.

"Tell me about yourself," Lee said, stroking her hair. "I want to know everything."

Patricia stirred so that she could look at him in surprise. This wasn't the kind of intimacy she had expected from him. It wasn't the sort of opening that usually came with casual sex. She squashed the idea that he might be thinking about something more. That would be ridiculous.

"I grew up in Green Valley," she said finally. "A country girl to the heart. I went to the twin cities for college, took some dance classes, got a teaching degree, had to come running back."

"You studied dance?"

Patricia wasn't sure how she should take the surprise in his voice. "Not that you'd know it from our dancing this evening, I know," she laughed sheepishly, choosing humor over getting offended, though it occurred to her that it would be easy to take his words the other way. "I don't have the figure for it, of course, but I love the art."

Lee was quiet, so Patricia had to fill the silence with something or think too hard about what couldn't possibly be.

"I started the Hands and Hearts Preschool after a few years of teaching middle school. There's not much of a market for it, of course—I've only got eight full-time students this year, and that's two more than last. It doesn't do much more than hire Andrea and pay the classroom rent, so I waitress on the side. I'd make more at Hardy's, but the skirts they make the staff wear there wouldn't reflect well on being a preschool teacher, so I work at the cafe."

She was babbling about *money* again, Patricia realized. Before she could stop herself, she had asked, "What about you? You aren't just a construction worker with McDonald Company."

# Chapter Ten

LEE TRIED NOT TO SQUIRM. He had known this question was coming, and he wasn't sure how to handle it. Money was one of those tricky subjects that seemed to embarrass her when she brought it up, and while he knew that she didn't have much of her own, he knew that earning her own was a matter of pride. "No," he admitted.

"So... you own it?"

"No, I own the company that owns it."

Patricia thought about that. "That's some conglomerate, right? D.C.L? D.M.L?"

"D.L.C. Contracting," Lee said, then added. "And no, I own the company that owns that. Also, a factory in Milwaukee and a small financial firm in Duluth."

"Oh," Patricia said dryly. "Only a *small* financial firm, though."

Lee did squirm then, relishing the feeling of her bare skin against his as he did. "Well, medium-sized, I suppose. Large for Duluth, maybe."

Patricia buried her face in the pillow and Lee was alarmed when her shoulders began shaking. Was she angry? He put a tentative hand on her shoulder, and she lifted her face from the pillow to let a whoop of laughter out.

Bemused, Lee watched as she chortled with abandon, laughing until tears rolled down her cheeks. "I had no idea financial firms were so entertaining," he said, mystified, and he recognized that he was frowning at her.

"They aren't," Patricia agreed, wiping her cheeks. The exertion of sex and laughter made her face glow. "It's just... I..."

She had to smother her hoots of laughter in the pillow again, while Lee helplessly patted her, not sorry for the excuse to keep his hands on her. He eventually had to laugh with her, even though he wasn't sure of the joke.

She finally managed to get her breath under control and told him, eyes dancing, "I brought you scholarship paperwork."

Lee felt dim. "Scholarship paperwork?" She wanted him to sponsor a scholarship?

"Well," Patricia explained, looking sheepish now. "You drove that beat up truck, and Clara was wearing short pants and no boots. I thought you might have trouble covering the tuition."

Lee cast his memory back. Clara had been so adamant about her choice of pants and shoes that first day. He hadn't considered that they had been her favorites for some time, and that she had grown in that time and that although they were clean, and hadn't been cheap, they were starting to look worn. "I let Clara pick her own clothes," he explained, sounding more defensive than he meant.

"It's okay," Patricia said hastily. "Most kids have favorites! You just... don't look like a millionaire, you know." She propped up on an elbow and gave him a stern look that was belied by her dancing eyes. "And you don't tip like one, either. 15%? *Really*?"

Lee put his hands behind his head and played along with a lofty sniff. "I'm not a millionaire, I'm a billionaire. And I should have tipped 10%. We had to wait a good five minutes for a refill on that milk we spilled."

"You're lucky I didn't land that second glass in your lap," Patricia countered with a sniff of her own.

"You could have licked it up, if you had," Lee suggested. "That would have gotten you a better tip."

Patricia giggled and sat up so she could hit him with the pillow. "Dirty mind!"

The pillow hit was all the invitation that Lee need to sit up and wrestle her back down onto the bed with kisses and caresses. Patricia kissed back, unquenched passion in her mouth and hands, until she had to break away from him in giggles again.

"What's so funny?" Lee asked, kissing her ear.

"Harriette Ambler!"

Lee pulled away in puzzlement. "What about her?"

"She fancies herself the local robber baron," Patricia explained. "She works in real estate, and she's going to be devastated to realize that she's a pauper compared to you."

Lee shuddered. "That horrible woman with the bright purple Chrysler and the impractical shoes."

"That's the one. I hope she decides being second best in a town this small is intolerable and leaves before she does more damage here."

"Damage? More than being an eyesore with that car?"

Some of the life unexpectedly drained out of Patricia–everything about her was so irrepressibly expressive that Lee could practically read her moods in the pores of her skin.

"I mentioned she was in real estate," she explained sadly. "She specializes in selling off historical properties to developers. She has aspirations of making Green Valley a bedroom community for Milwaukee. There's talk that she's buying old Gertie's farm to put in a membership warehouse, and she's trying to buy the schoolhouse I rent."

"I'm a developer," Lee reminded her, driven to honesty by Patricia's transparent distress. "But turning Green Valley into a sea of cheap apartments and box stores is an appalling idea." He didn't have to exaggerate his reaction.

Patricia's head tilted as she focused a thoughtful gaze on him. "You didn't bulldoze this old place to build something new and perfect."

"I love old buildings," Lee explained. "And I moved here so that Clara could grow up in a small town, not an extended city suburb. I want to build her a treehouse, and let her run wild in the woods when she's older." If Clara was a shifter like he was, that would be more important than he could easily explain.

"I hope Green Valley still is that small, quiet town when she's older," Patricia said, settling back into the pillows.

"I could make sure that it is," Lee was spurred to declare. "I can keep developers from buying any more here, and stop construction on anything that's in progress. There are some restoration projects two towns over that could suddenly need the company resources more urgently. If they aren't mine, I know people who can get them moved. I know the company owners of two of the major membership warehouses and could convince them to look elsewhere for their expansions."

Patricia sat up again, astonished eyes dancing and a new, hopeful smile tugging at her lips. "You can DO that?"

Lee gave a practiced nonchalant smile. "It's done."

"I never thought I'd find that kind of power sexy," Patricia said, new laughter in her voice.

"But..." Lee prompted her.

Patricia rolled onto her hands and knees and growled playfully through her loose hair, "It's the sexiest thing I've ever heard in my life. Roar!"

The growl, and her seductive look, brought his bear roaring to the surface, and Lee growled in reply before he could stop himself. If anything, she looked aroused by his response, and snapped her teeth suggestively at him. He could no longer keep his hands off of her, and reached out to gather her close.

# Chapter Eleven

PATRICIA TUMBLED INTO Lee's arms with delight, relishing the strength in his shoulders and arms. He lifted her to straddle him with ease, and she could already feel him engorging again, his thick member rising to brush the insides of her thighs as she playfully nibbled at his neck and ears.

He rumbled right back at her, and his hands at her waist pulled her closer, until he was teasing her entrance. Before he claimed her, though, he rolled her over so that he was spanning her, kissing her neck and her jaw, keeping himself tantalizingly just out of reach as he caressed her skin and bit at her collarbone as if he were barely in control of himself.

Patricia groaned and caught herself clawing at his shoulders desperately–she couldn't think around the desire that was welling up in her. She writhed, pressing her hips up at him, and he teased her more, pressing at her waiting, wet lips but not entering.

"Please..." she heard, and realized it was her own voice, rough and needy.

When he finally took possession of her, filling her deliciously, she had to bite her lip to keep from crying out in abandon. The taste of blood was iron on her tongue.

Then he was kissing it off of her, his tongue tangling with hers as he filled her and retreated, thrust after thrust, her orgasms a dizzy cascade of pleasure.

Lee stopped and withdrew abruptly, breathing hard and clawing the sheets. Patricia soothed him, stroking his sides and kissing his face while he regained control of himself. Impulsively, she tumbled him over and took the top position, precariously near the edge of the bed. She gasped as Lee took them one circle further, catching her and flipping her over to kneel in the plush carpet at the edge of the bed. She was sprawled leaning over the bed, and he was kneeling behind her, pressing irresistibly at her nether mouth. She was still unexpectedly hungry for him, even still hazy from her orgasms.

He pressed into her slick waiting lips with a little groan of passion, and they were moving together as one, relishing this new position of possession and release.

He came at last, just as Patricia discovered new heights of physical joy, and the sheets were dragged from the bed by their grasping hands.

For a long, gasping moment, they simply collapsed there beside the bed, tangled in sheets and sweat and the sweet fluids of their lovemaking. Slow hands trailed over each other; Patricia could not get enough of the hills and valleys of his muscles, even so fully sated as she was.

"And you think you aren't a dancer," Lee said near her ear, and there was something that Patricia couldn't identify in his voice.

She had to giggle, languidly, and answer, "I said everyone is a dancer at heart. Especially when the music is right." For now, the music was his heartbeat, hammering near her ear and rattling through her own body because they were so tightly entwined. He squeezed her breath away, then gently untangled her from the sheets and helped her up.

Patricia flowed up into his arms and kissed him, feeling graceful and liquid. "I noticed that your shower has two showerheads..." she suggested. She didn't want to stop touching him, and didn't, through an entire steamy shower. They soaped each other, and rinsed each other, and dried each other, carefully, then fell naked into bed where they snuggled in to snatch a few precious hours of sleep.

LEE WOKE TO AN ARMFUL of delight. His bear was as contented as he was, for the first time in a very long time, and he still felt deliciously sated after their active night.

Patricia stirred, and mumbled something into her pillow.

"Hmmm?" Lee asked her, cradling her close.

"Pancakes," Patricia repeated. "You promised pancakes and I'm *starving*!"

He was too, now that she had vocalized it, and it was possibly the only thing that could have driven him out of bed. He reluctantly let go of her and rolled out of bed.

Sunlight was streaming through the gap in the curtains, and Patricia put a pillow over her head when he opened them wide to look out. The snow had stopped during the night, and the entire world was blanketed with white, downy serenity.

"I think it snowed two feet," Lee said in wonder.

"Pancakes!" Patricia reminded him from underneath her pillow. She was probably used to snow.

If the snow didn't impress her, the pancakes did. Lee managed not to embarrass himself, mixing the ingredients and cooking them each on the skillet to golden perfection.

Patricia, dressed in her own jeans with one of Lee's big shirts belted over it, repeatedly expressed her delight, and ravenously downed a stack smothered with syrup.

"I told you they were good," Clara said smugly. But she had to be coaxed back to her chair to eat them several times—she was more enthralled by the snowy scenery out the window, and the prospect of playing in it.

They had barely put down their forks before she was dragging them to the door to go out, not even interested in making the bubbles to wash up.

But when the door finally closed behind them, Clara wasn't sure what to do, and she stood on the porch in her crinkling snowsuit blinking at the bright vista.

"Let's make a snowman!" Patricia suggested at once, and waded fearlessly out into the snow.

Clara took Lee's gloved hand and followed her, floundering in the tall snow. She helped roll up the snowman's base, and patted it carefully into shape, slowly taking the role of director as the snowman grew too tall for her to reach.

"The head is crooked!" she pointed out, after it had been heaved into place.

Patricia struggled to remedy that to his daughter's satisfaction, while Lee went back into the house to find a scarf and hat. "We need a carrot for the nose!" Clara called after him imperiously. "And coal for the eyes!"

"I don't think we have those things!" Lee warned her from the porch, but he gamely went inside to try to find them.

Cubed frozen carrots from a package of mixed vegetables weren't going to meet her demands, he decided, so he brought a piece of scrap trim for a nose and two washers from his workbench for eyes. An extra scarf from Clara's closet was obtained, and one of his own baseball hats, when he couldn't find an extra wool hat.

When he returned, Clara and Patricia were standing back from the snowman, looking at it critically. Lee's offerings were considered by his daughter carefully, and deemed acceptable.

The resulting snowman was still lopsided, but Clara gave a pleased smile, and agreed that he would do. "I like snow!" she told Lee seriously. "I want it to snow always!"

"I'm going to remind you that you said that someday, and you'll deny it," Lee predicted.

Patricia laughed, of course, and dragged Clara off to make snow angels.

The sound of their laughter together was impossibly familiar, like Lee had been waiting his entire life to hear it.

# Chapter Twelve

PATRICIA LOOKED UP at the sky, sweeping her arms to make angel wings in the fluffy snowbank.

"Like this?" asked Clara.

Patricia had to struggle to sit up in the loose snow. "That's perfect, Honey! She looks beautiful!"

"How do I get uuuuppppp?" Clara wailed, giggling and thrashing.

Chuckling, Patricia went to help her up, then tossed her, shrieking with laughter, into another snowbank, then dived in after her. Laughing and swimming through the snow together, Patricia tickled her and rolled her in hugs.

They lay cuddled together for a long moment once their laughter had worn out.

"Do you think my Momma is an angel now?" Clara asked, unexpectedly.

"I bet she is," Patricia said carefully, sitting up with her. "The most beautiful angel ever."

"She was beautiful," Clara agreed. "I've seen pictures."

Patricia glanced over to where Lee, out of earshot, was clearing off her car and shoveling around it. "You don't remember her?"

"She died when I was a baby," Clara said gravely. "She was sick for a long time and they couldn't make her okay."

Patricia hugged her tight. "I'm sure she loved you very much and was sad to go."

"Papa was very sad, too," Clara observed, and Patricia had no answer for that.

They sat together in the snow for some time, watching Lee together. Far away, there was the grating sound of big equipment along the road. "What's that?" Clara asked.

'The sound of the end to my winterland fantasy,' Patricia didn't say out loud. "That's the snowplows! They are down there clearing all the snow off of the roads so that it's safe to drive again!" It was already above freezing, and the snow was warm and soft. Perfect for... "You know what we should do?" she said quietly near Clara's ear.

The little girl froze, sensing a conspiracy. "What?"

Patricia made a snowball in her gloved hands and looked suggestively at Lee, whose back was to them.

"Oh!" Clara said loudly, then clapped a mittened hand over her mouth. Over it, her eyes danced in anticipation and she nodded.

Together, they made a small arsenal of snowballs, gathered in Patricia's hat. If Lee noticed their preparations, he gamely pretended not to, so that when they staged their attack with a warrior's whoop and a flurry of ill-aimed snowballs, he was taken entirely by surprise and staggered back under the onslaught.

Patricia got at least a few good snowballs to hit him, and a few of Clara's landed close enough to splash him as they fell apart.

"I'm under attack!" he hollered gamely, pretending to be mortally wounded. "Yetis from the north with their deadly snowballs!" Undeterred, he scooped up an answering round of snowballs, hitting gently, but with far more precision at Clara's shoulders. She laughed and ran behind the car. Patricia ducked one that would have hit her face, and returned one to his chest, exploding in powder.

As she retreated behind the car with Clara, Lee called, "Get her, Clara!" and the traitor unleashed an enthusiastic rain of tiny snowballs on her unexpectedly.

"Whose side are you on?" she demanded, turning back to find herself cornered by Lee. She couldn't help giggling and being a little deliciously terrified as he descended on her, sweeping her up in his arms and tossing her into a snowbank with ease. "I won't go down easy!" she protested, and she tossed a snowball right into his face as she laughed and struggled up.

Clara danced around at his feet. "Toss me, Papa! Toss me!"

Lee obliged, then gave each of them a hand as the rumbling machinery in the distance grew louder, and a truck with a plow and the markings of Lee's business appeared at the curve of the driveway, pushing a modest wall of snow before it. Clara took each of their hands as Patricia tried to smooth down her parka and look a little less like she had just been rolling in the snow with unprofessional abandon.

"Do you have to go now?" Clara asked, carefully pulling them back from the big truck.

Patricia met Lee's eyes briefly and had to look away. "Yes, Sweetie," she said, trying to mask her regret. "It's time for me to go to my home now that the road is clear."

Clara let go of Lee's hand to wrap both of her arms around Patricia's knees. "I hope you come back soon," she said mournfully.

"So do I," said Lee, unexpectedly, and Patricia looked up into his face in surprise and sudden joy.

"Well," she said, smiling slowly. "I'll need to return your shirt."

# Chapter Thirteen

PATRICIA DUMPED THE blocks back into the big bin, enjoying the noisy percussion over the radio that was playing refreshingly grown-up music as she and Andrea cleaned up the room and prepped for the next day's work.

"I'm so glad you took my advice," Andrea said smugly, tossing another stray block from where she was sweeping behind the craft tables.

"Which advice was that?" Patricia feigned innocence.

"The advice about Clara's gorgeous dad," Andrea said, not fooled. "Look at you! You haven't been this happy and relaxed since you opened this circus!" Another block arced to follow the first into the bin.

"I probably shouldn't," Patricia confessed, smiling foolishly and denying nothing. "It's not exactly professional..."

Andrea snorted. "It's not like you're *his* teacher," she said dismissively. "And it's not like you were even chasing him like half the rest of this town, either."

Patricia found that she was hugging the teddy bear she had just picked up and put it back on the bench with the others before she could indulge in dancing around with it. "No, but..."

"No buts!" Andrea said, flinging another block across the room. This one missed and bounced onto the floor. "You deserve a little happiness," Andrea said emphatically.

"Well, keep quiet about it," Patricia said. "I'm sure it will be over with the semester, and the last thing I want to do is give those harpies more to gossip about."

"Too late for that," Andrea said with no sympathy. "Mrs. Harrison saw you leaving his place last week, and told her hairdresser, who told Sabrina, so now everyone knows. You should have seen the way Harriette was glaring at you when she left with Trevor."

"Uuuugggghhhh," Patricia moaned. "I was hoping not to get *her* attention."

"She's got to have some vent for her frustration. Sabrina says that her real estate deals are falling through like it's going out of fashion, and she's lost buckets of money because Gertie wouldn't sell. So what have you found out about Clara's mother?" Andrea dumped her dustpan into the trash and came to lean in towards Patricia conspiratorially.

If the idea of Harriette's jealousy had left Patricia feeling cold, the mention of Lee's dead wife left her chest aching. "She died when Clara was a baby, and she was sick. That's all I know." It was a lie of omission. She also knew Lee still loved her.

"You haven't found anything other than that out in nearly a month?" Andrea scoffed, clearly not impressed with her investigative skills.

"Lee doesn't really want to talk about her, and it's not an easy subject to bring up with him. Not that we're doing a lot of... talking."

Andrea giggled in appreciation for that, and then suggested, "What about Clara? Doesn't she know anything about her mother?"

"Are you really suggesting I pump a four-year-old for information?"

Andrea's green eyes sparkled with mischief. "Why else even be a preschool teacher? The little devils are ripe for providing the very best in high grade gossip. Wave a cookie in front of their nose, and they'll bring you all the skeletons from the closets."

Patricia clipped the lid onto the last toy bin and shoved it into place. "You're unbelievable, Andrea," she said with a reluctant laugh.

"Fine, fine," Andrea said, returning the broom to its corner and flipping the switch for the overhead lights. "I'll have to do my own investigation, then."

"Have fun, Sherlock," Patricia retorted. "But don't drag me into your sordid curiosity!"

She turned off the last lights and pulled the door shut behind her. She was curious, yes, but the ghost of Angela was too painful to face, knowing that Lee still loved her.

PATRICIA HAD ALL BUT forgotten Andrea's threat to investigate, so she was surprised when Andrea pressed two printouts into her hands during a lull in the preschool set up. At first, it made no sense to her. The first was a flyer for a prestigious ballet, a waifish figure in white standing on toe. The name, Angel Barrette, meant nothing to Patricia.

"What's this?"

"That's Clara's mother," Andrea said, something like smugness at the corners of her mouth.

Patricia blinked and looked again. Angel —— Angela – was the perfect ballerina, all swan-graceful and delicate strength, and she was headlining the flyer for a prestigious company show at an uptown stage that even country-girl Patricia had heard of. Patricia swallowed and found that her grip was beginning to crinkle the edge of the printout. She flipped to the next page, a tearful obituary for a beloved wife and mother, famous dancer, darling daughter, and, from Patricia's swift skim, well-named Angel.

"I found her on the Internet," Andrea said. "Took some digging, let me tell you. Different last name, most of her stories are about her gazillionaire daddy and his stock-topping companies. Which, by the way, when were you going to tell me that your boyfriend was a billionaire?"

"He's not my boyfriend," Patricia replied automatically. Her heart was sitting in the bottom of her stomach. She'd never thought that Lee was particularly serious about her, but she never thought he might be comparing her to *this*. Angela was perfect. The obituary made her sound like a saint. She volunteered for charitable events, and there were testimonies from her fellow dancers that she was dedicated and talented, never using her family connections for unfair advantage. A husband, Leland, and a baby, were bare mentions.

She thought about sliding around barefoot in Lee's empty dining room, teaching them both to dance, and felt like a fraud. A giant, clumsy, curvy, fraud.

How could he let her make a fool of herself that way? How could he sit there and let her gush on about dancing, when he knew that what she was doing was some backwoods country chicken dance compared to what he was used to?

"Patricia? Honey?" Andrea's voice was anxious, and seemed to be a hundred miles away.

Patricia very carefully put the papers down on her desk and stood up, grateful when the bell at the front door gave its cheerful jangle. "The students are coming," she said, shoving aside the turmoil in her belly. "Let's get to work."

Patricia had never been so glad for a busy day in her life. The children were fractious, and there were more messes and accidents to clean up than usual, giving her a good excuse to put her head down and work hard, ignoring Andrea's worried looks and her own heart for the scissors and glue of the classroom.

# Chapter Fourteen

"NO, NO, I'M SURE," Lee said, glad that he was on the phone and not at the office in person. He knew he was smiling foolishly, and he couldn't seem to help himself, but the topic and the person at the other end of the line were anything but a smiling matter.

"This is a big deal, Lee," Dan told him, puzzlement clear in his voice even with the shaky cell connection they were on.

"You have no idea how big," Lee agreed. "But it means a lot to me, and you know I'll turn you a good favor down the road."

"I trust you," Dan finally said reluctantly. "But it means a lot of changes in our production schedule while we find another suitable property. They're going to want a good reason for this at headquarters."

"Tell them it was an Indian burial ground," Lee said flippantly. "Or that you struck quicksand."

There was a moment of silence. "Did you just make a joke?" Dan asked incredulously.

Lee wondered if Dan could hear the grin on his face. "No, I don't do that," he said, as seriously as he could muster. "Just tell them the real estate agent was wearing impractical shoes and you couldn't strike a deal."

"I think that little country town has gotten under your skin," Dan said, and he chuckled. "Every woman wears impractical shoes."

Lee thought about Patricia, sliding barefoot around in his dining room with her big, clunky snow boots by his door. "Not every woman," he said. When they hung up, he slipped the little box he'd been toying with out of his pocket. It was black velvet, and he flipped it open with one thumb to check the contents again. It wasn't a huge glittering diamond like the one he'd given Angela, but he couldn't picture anything like that on Patricia's practical hands. This was a simple band, in braided shades of gold, with chips of rubies and diamond flush with the surface; nothing that would snag on craft supplies or mittens.

He would ask her tonight–, tomorrow morning, over pancakes. He'd let Clara help him with the proposal, then that afternoon during her nap, he would come clean with Patricia about being a shape-shifter. Maybe the ring on her finger would help her accept it a little more easily if he explained how it came with the idea of a mate.

He snapped the box shut and put it back in his pocket, picking up his phone instead. There were more calls to be made, and then there was something else he was finally ready to do.

PATRICIA COULD NOT get the picture of Angel out of her head. She toyed with the idea of canceling her evening with Lee, but couldn't find a good enough excuse. Besides, though her heart ached, the rest of her longed to be with him. She yearned for him in a way that she'd never desired another man. Every time they made love, she felt more connected and closer than she'd ever been to anyone, and it filled some hollow inside her that she'd never recognized was there.

She paused, with her hand raised to knock at the front door, in a moment of unexpected clarity. She loved him. It wasn't just that she wanted and lusted after him, she loved him, to the bottom of her heart, and she wasn't sure what to do with the overwhelming emotional backlash of that realization.

Clara opened the door before she could collect herself enough to knock or turn and flee, and Patricia forced herself out of her daze to smile down at the adorable girl.

"I saw you drive up!" Clara sang, bouncing forward to grab one of her hands, careless of her bare feet in the snow on the porch. "Papa said you would read me a story before bed!"

Patricia had just enough time to kick of her snow boots before Clara was pulling her up the stairs by one hand. "Alright, alright," Patricia had to laugh helplessly.

Lee was standing at the top of the stairs with small pink slippers, looking harried and handsome. "You aren't supposed to go outside barefoot," he told Clara, but his eyes were only on Patricia, and he smiled in a way that made her toes tingle.

'Don't fall for this man,' Patricia reminded herself, far too late, and then she was being swept down the hallway towards Clara's room.

To her surprise, framed photographs now lined one wall. Clara was pulling her along too fast to look closely at them; she only got glimpses of a stately ancient collection of grim-faced ancestors in furs and jewels, giving way to more modern tinted prints and finally color plates.

"This is my mother," Clara said with unexpected gravity, pausing only at the last pieces. There were several that Patricia recognized now as the dancer from Andrea's printout. One was a formal dance portrait, with a dramatically lit stage and a slight figure in classical tutu and pointe pose. The next photograph was a light-haired woman in a fur coat seated at the edge of a fountain holding a bundled baby. Lee, looking younger, was smiling over her shoulder. Golden sunlight sparkled in the water and made a halo around the woman's head. She really did look like an angel.

"She's beautiful," Patricia said, honestly, hoping her heartbreak wouldn't be heard in her voice. This was a woman no one could hope to compare to, especially not a country cow like herself. She steeled herself to stick to her plan. This night was a final goodbye. She had to get out before she lost too much of herself to a perfect dream she could never really be a part of.

Clara seemed to accept her statement as fact, and said cheerfully, "Let's go read *Give a Mouse a Cookie!*"

That, with the careful scrutiny of every page and all the hugs and blanket arrangements required, took all of Patricia's attention until the door latched behind them, and she and Lee were once again standing together in the hallway.

This time, however, she could feel the oblique attention of Angela's portrait, judging her from a swan-perfect pose.

If Lee had tried to kiss her there, she might have balked, but he only took her hand, tenderly, and led her further down the hallway, past the end of the portraits, to his room.

"Patricia," he started to say, but she couldn't handle words.

Instead, she reached up and put arms around his neck, kissing him with all the love and passion he had ignited in her. If she was going to say goodbye to him tonight, she was going to do it properly, and put this all behind her when she left in the morning.

# Chapter Fifteen

LEE HAD CHANGED HIS mind again. He couldn't wait to ask Patricia to marry him, he would ask her tonight, so that he could get past the terrible looming reveal. And he couldn't ask her to marry him until she knew the full truth about him, so he had to... had to...

Any plans he had made unraveled and fell apart when she put insistent arms around his neck and kissed him like the world was ending.

The feeling of her body against him, strong and yielding and so perfectly rounded in all the right places left him unable to form words, even if her mouth had allowed it. He slipped arms around her, and kissed back.

They undressed each other slowly, not willing to break the kiss more than was required for pulling shirts off and maneuvering tricky zippers and belts. Lee didn't think he was imagining the different tenor to their dance–less laughter and enthusiasm and more desperation. Did she know, somehow, what he had planned? A trickle of doubt crept in–would she be able to handle the knowledge of his shifter side? What if she didn't want to marry him... then she was putting tender hands on either side of his face and murmuring as she rested her forehead against his. His bear, with none of his own inner doubts, knew what to do with his mate, so close, and so naked, and so did his body.

He lifted her onto the bed with another kiss, his hard member pressing at her lower mouth, but not demanding entrance, only reminding her of his presence.

His attention was for her lips and mouth, swollen already with his kisses, and her beautiful face–every freckle beloved. He wanted to tell her how much he loved her, but his mouth was busy, kissing the line of her jaw and the edge of her ear. He nibbled at her lobe, and she writhed below him, pressing upward at him with a low moan.

He held himself back and kissed down her neck, finding pale skin that rarely saw sunlight, and the fine blonde hairs that had escaped the braid she was wearing today. Her arching collarbones got his attention next, feathered with kisses and licks as he finally let himself explore down her chest to the breasts that were quivering below.

Patricia gave a musical breath of desire and pleasure, arching into his questing mouth. She was so woman, so full and waiting and wanting, and her breasts were big, beautiful handfuls and mouthfuls of joy. He nibbled and kissed and licked, and she gasped and groaned and tangled her hands in his hair.

Finally, when their desire was at a fever pitch Lee had not thought was possible, he let himself enter her, finding solace and relief and raw animal need at the sensation of being buried deep inside of her.

They finished together, almost musically, and lay entwined while their heartbeats slowly returned to normal.

Lee felt completed, as if his entire life had been a song waiting for its harmony, and now she sang with him.

"Patricia," he said, brushing her hair back from her face when he'd finally caught enough of his breath. "I have something I need to tell you."

Silence answered him, and a glance told him, unexpectedly, that she was asleep, long eyelashes splayed over her cheeks.

Lee found himself smiling and snuggled closer. He wasn't worried about what she would do anymore. Whatever happened, she was his mate, and he could be patient. He fell into the easiest sleep he could ever remember, and dreamed at once of wandering the woods with a golden bear at his side.

# Chapter Sixteen

PATRICIA WOKE SLOWLY, comfortably sore and clinging to sleep as long as she could. She was warm and safe, curled up against something plush and large. She wiggled closer, not wanting to wake up and face the inevitable goodbye, and recognized through a fog that it didn't exactly feel *plush*, but coarser, and longer, and it was larger than a pillow or a person. She wrinkled her brow in confusion, the unexpected discovery waking her further. She was in bed with a fur coat? Even breaths raised the bulk beneath her out-flung arm, and she realized with alarm that it was too big to be Lee, even if he had, for some bizarre reason, gotten up in the middle of the night to put on a large buffalo coat.

She withdrew her arm cautiously, rolling away with care, and raised her head enough to see, in the early dawn light coming through the window, that there was a bear sprawled across the bed, enormous head on a pillow, sheets tangled in its back paws.

As collected as Patricia liked to consider herself, the shock drove a scream from her lips before she could remind herself that waking it was probably a bad idea.

The mountain of bear snorted and rumbled, and Patricia, naked, propelled herself back out of the bed and cast around helplessly for a weapon of some kind, any kind. Bereft of anything useful, she leapt for the curtain rod over the big window, and managed to pull it down with a crash as the bear woke and rose, blinking sleepy eyes at her from its vantage on the bed. Could she make a break past it for the door without it intercepting her? Patricia wondered. And where the hell was Lee?

Even as she summoned that thought, struggling to rip off the curtains that were weighing down the curtain rod she was trying to use as a makeshift weapon, the bear made a strangled noise of alarm and surprise.

That was it, Patricia realized. It was awake now for good, and she was armed with a crappy brass curtain rod and a few yards of white tapestry. She was going to be bear breakfast, and the curtains were going to be completely ruined from the blood. At least she wouldn't have to go through the ordeal of saying goodbye to Lee...

From down the hall, undoubtedly wakened by the racket they were making, Clara's shrill scream pierced the scene. The bear's head pivoted towards the door, and Patricia leapt for it without thinking. She was naked, and didn't think the curtain rod would survive one good blow from the bear's paws, but she wasn't about to let it go after Clara. Her only hope was to frighten it off, so she gave a blood-curdling warcry and jumped onto the bed with her curtain rod raised above her.

It was caught by a hand–a human hand–and somehow, through a blur that Patricia couldn't follow, it was Lee kneeling on the bed before her; the bear was nowhere to be seen.

"Patricia! Patricia, it's okay! It's me! I'm sorry, I've been wanting to tell you..."

Patricia's pulse hammered in her ears, adrenaline coursing through her like fire. "Tell me what?" she managed. "Bear. There was a bear..."

"That was me," Lee said, ridiculously. "I'm the bear. I'm sorry, I didn't want to surprise you like that. I must have done it in my sleep. I was just... comfortable."

Patricia stared. "You were... comfortable? You know, most people, when they get really comfortable, they accidentally fart or something. They don't... turn into bears."

Lee blinked at her, then burst out laughing.

Patricia tried to maintain her stern visage and failed in the face of his laughter, falling forward with limbs that were suddenly utterly weak and shaking, face first into the bed, howling with hysterical laughter.

"Papa?" Clara's frightened voice and timid knock from outside of the door made them both sit up and silence their laughter.

"It's okay, kitten!" Lee said at once. "Nothing's wrong. I just..."

"Farted!" they said together, giggling like loons.

Clara was silent outside the door for a moment. "You woke me up! We have to make pancakes now! I'm getting dressed!" she said accusingly, and then they heard her little footsteps stomping back away down the hallway.

Lee rolled out of his side of the bed and grabbed the clothing that waited there. "You heard the little tyrant," he said, then sobered. "I did want to tell you a little less... uh..."

"Alarmingly?" Patricia suggested. "In a less heart-attack in-ducing fashion?" As weird as it seemed, now that the adrena-line was ebbing away, the idea of Lee being a shapeshifter was somehow comfortable. It was a tiny affirmation of all the mag-ic she had clung to believing in since she was a small girl, and it suited Lee. All of his serious demeanor and secrecy, all of his riches and his enormous palace of a house; it fit that he was a shapechanger prince from a fairy tale.

'And you aren't a princess,' Patricia reminded herself, sor-rowfully, pulling on her jeans and t-shirt. "So, is it some kind of curse or something?" she asked, as if it was perfectly ordinary.

"No," Lee said slowly, shaking his head. "I come from a line of shifters. There are a lot of around. I picked this town because it's usually... friendly to our type."

"That... explains some things," Patricia said, thinking about some of the odd people she knew at the diner, and the way she sometimes felt like there were topics that went silent when she approached, and so many of the stories she heard as a child that she had dismissed as fantasy.

"There's something else," Lee said hesitantly, coming around the end of the bed. He was wearing his pants, but not his shirt, and Patricia looked at his sculpted chest instead of his dear face, bracing herself for the rest.

# Chapter Seventeen

AS REVEALS WENT, LEE suspected that it could have gone better. Still, Patricia seemed to be taking the shock in stride. She hadn't jumped out of the window, at least, and once the hysterical giggling had passed, she seemed to be surprisingly accepting of the whole thing.

"There's something else." Lee made himself keep going, knowing that if he lost momentum with this whole confession, it was only going to be harder.

Patricia made a conversational noise as she buttoned her shirt, smoothing the front down over her luscious breasts.

"Shifters... we have this thing, a mate, a *soulmate*. There's one person we're meant to be with, one perfect partner, that we–"

"I know." There was a serene smile on Patricia's face, still and deep, with an odd flavor that Lee couldn't put his finger on.

"It's just... this mate–"

"It's okay," she interrupted him swiftly. "I understand. I... already knew."

Relief flooded through Lee. Of course she knew. She had to know. How could she not have felt the incredible bond that they shared. He smiled, suspecting it was a ridiculously soppy smile, but he couldn't help it. "I'm so glad," he said simply.

"Clara's expecting pancakes," Patricia reminded him. She was so delightfully down-to-earth.

Lee swept up his shirt. "Yes! Pancakes!" He would stick to the original plan. A ring with her pancakes, and he'd have Clara there for the moment; all of the most precious people in his life together at once.

He rehearsed the moment in his head as they walked down the stairs to the kitchen, and imagined the words and Clara's laughter as he mixed up the pancake batter and heated the griddle. He was wrapped up in his busy mind until he brought the first stack of cakes to the table–and found Clara setting it for two.

"Where is Miss Patricia?" he asked, suddenly aware that she wasn't there, that he couldn't sense her nearby.

Clara looked at him with big blue eyes, alarmed at his surprise. "She drove away!"

Lee let the plate of pancakes fall the last few inches to the table and land with a clatter. "When? Where?"

"In her car!" Clara supplied helpfully. "She said she had to go."

Lee ran the distance to the front door in a matter of seconds, but the car was long gone, tracks in the snow showing her hasty escape. He stood there with the door open, cold air swirling over his bare feet. The sound of a car near the tree-shrouded bottom of the driveway gave him a moment of hope, but it moved away down the road.

He'd read her wrong. Finding out he was a shifter had changed her mind about him. Mate or not, she didn't want the complication that he was in her life. This was their goodbye then; a cold, empty driveway and uneaten pancakes. Lee stood there until Clara drew him back inside by the knees, complaining of the cold that he didn't even feel anymore.

PATRICIA FLEW DOWN the driveway much faster than she knew she should, trusting her Subaru to stick to the road and power her through the wet, drifting snow.

"I ought to have waited for the snowplows," she thought to herself, pulling out into the slushy, snowy road with the barest hint of a pause at the bottom of the driveway.

The snow had cleared and the clouds lifted, but given the tears that clouded her vision, Patricia knew she should pull over. She slowed to a safer speed, but there was no clear shoulder here in the hills. She wiped her face with the back of her coat sleeve, biting back a sob.

If she had doubted that Lee was still in love with his dead wife, his words had erased that.

A *soulmate*, a perfect partner.

She couldn't compete with that.

She turned the defroster higher as the window began fogging in the cold and she realized it wasn't all her own tears obscuring her view. Behind her, headlights through the snow she was kicking up showed a car coming right up on her tail, driving close in the poor conditions.

Distracted from her own thoughts, Patricia scowled at the other car in the mirror, dark in the poor morning light. It wasn't driving well for the winding road, and was crawling up at her trunk without care for the slippery conditions. She tapped the brakes just enough to light up her taillights in warning but not to slow, and was equal parts alarmed and relieved when they backed off just a little and pulled into the oncoming lane–it was a stupid move in a place with no shoulder and no clear line of sight to traffic that might be coming from ahead, but at least she wouldn't have them tailing her all the way into town.

"Idiot," she muttered to herself, slowing to give them the best chance they could around the curve.

She was looking forward, focused on looking ahead for oncoming traffic and keeping her Subaru in its indistinct lane as the dark car passed, throwing snow into her windshield.

Momentarily blinded, Patricia went too far into the soft snow at the edge, and lost whatever control she'd had. Tires spun in the soft snow, and her car tottered at the crest of the shoulder before finally plummeting into the ditch beyond. For a moment Patricia thought she could simply ride down, hoping against hope that she wouldn't hit a big tree at the bottom, but it was too steep, too slippery, and the world went into a crazy spin as the car finally rolled down into oblivion, the airbag exploding into her and slamming her back into the seat.

# Chapter Eighteen

LEE TRIED NOT TO MOPE, eating too many pancakes with Clara and feeling the burn of the jewelry box in his pocket. His daughter, at least, seemed oblivious to the fact that everything had gone perfectly sideways, and chattered gleefully about imaginary friends, and her plans for the weekend, which seemed to involve a ball with a prince, a baseball game, and a big party for her stuffed animals, all hosted in the swimming pool, apparently.

He was carrying the dirty dishes to the sink, not even cheered by Clara's requests to make the bubbles, when the doorbell rang.

He almost dropped the plates, and Clara went scampering for the front door.

"Slow down, kitten!" he cautioned her, putting the plates down on the counter before he followed her. Relief flooded him. Patricia had come back. She had just needed a little space to get used to the idea, and let the whole crazy idea of shifters and soulmates settle in.

Clara got to the door just before him, and flung it open. They both froze, confronted by the entirely unexpected sight of Patricia's preschool assistant Andrea, standing naked on the porch with her arms wrapped ineffectively around herself.

"Patricia needs your help!" she demanded, with no explanation of her nudity or how she'd gotten there–there was no car in the driveway behind her.

Lee only stared for a moment before moving aside so that she could come in. "I... uh..." There was no standard greeting for naked women in snow.

"You are not the only shifter in town," Andrea said dryly. "Though you may be the most unobservant."

"I'm... uh... sorry?" Lee grabbed the closest thing that might fit her, waffling a moment between Clara's little coat and his own quilted flannel shirt. The first might actually be closer to her diminutive size. He decided on the flannel, suspecting she'd prefer more cover.

Andrea took it in stride. "I know that I was always around a powerful distraction," she shrugged, accepting the shirt. "But *she* is in trouble now."

Shock gave way to a calm readiness. Whatever his mate needed, Lee could feel his bear preparing to supply it; it felt like adrenaline, but more focused. "What happened?"

"She drove off the road," Andrea said, a glint of anger in her golden eyes. "I was flying over and saw the whole thing. A car passed her on a blind corner, and she veered into a ditch about a mile just down the road."

"You left her there?"

Lee didn't think about how accusatory he sounded until Andrea rebutted angrily, "I couldn't get the door open, and I wasn't doing her much good, naked in the snow. I'm a hawk, not a bear."

Moving automatically, Lee was already pulling on his boots and shrugging into a parka with purpose.

"It's the curve past the guardrail right before town," Andrea said, nodding decisively at him.

"Clara, stay here with Miss Andrea," Lee commanded with a growl, reaching for his truck keys.

Clara had born witness to their odd exchange with eyes like saucers, certain something was afoot, but not sure what to do with it. She looked trustingly at Andrea, not in the slightest bothered by the fact that she had arrived naked, and nodded. She darted for one swift hug from her father, her arms wrapping briefly around Lee's leg. When Lee knelt to hug her back, she solemnly said, "Make Miss Patricia be okay."

It was that simple, in Lee's mind. He was going to go get Patricia and make her be okay. Even if she wanted nothing to do with him now that she knew his shifter secret, he had to save her. "You bet, cub."

Then he was out the door, bolting for the truck.

Behind him, Clara fixed Andrea with a curious gaze. "Can I make bubbles for the dishes?" she asked.

# Chapter Nineteen

PATRICIA WOKE SLOWLY, aware first that her hands were cold. She moved to tuck them under her blanket, then realized that she wasn't in her own bed, that she was suspended by seatbelt straps upside down in the crushed cab of her car. Something on the dashboard was beeping weakly. Anger gave her false warmth as she remembered the dark car that had foolishly passed her, and she struggled out of the seatbelt before she could suspect she might be injured and possibly shouldn't move before she had determined the extent of her damage. Pain radiated from her left ankle, and the ache in her shoulders made her suspect she would find that she was black and blue, but Patricia's quick assessment was that she didn't have anything worse than a sprained ankle.

She wiggled it experimentally and had to bite back a cry. Maybe a broken ankle.

She righted herself in the wrong-side-up cab, and began to struggle with the car door.

The latch still moved, but the metal was crushed into a form that didn't allow it to open, despite Patricia straining against it with all her strength and weight. Somehow, the glass was still in place, though it and the windshield had shattered in place. She'd have to break out of one of the windows, she decided, winded, but the idea made her ankle throb. She found one of her gloves, which had been in the passenger seat, and switched them between her cold hands, trying to decide which would be easier to get out of. The enclosed space of the car was beginning to make her feel trapped.

She curled up on the upside-down roof of the car and closed her eyes, feeling tears well up. She took a deep breath, trying to damp down her terror and think of something peaceful. Lee's face came to her imagination immediately, and the feeling of his arms around her. She pushed it aside fiercely, reminding herself that the relationship was not going anywhere. He'd had his perfect partner already, and she opened her eyes, prepared to kick out the front windshield with her good foot.

Suddenly, Lee's face wasn't just in her imagination, but at her door, worry in every line of his face. "Get back," he yelled through the glass, and she obediently backed as far as she could into the inverted roof of the passenger seat.

Through the frosted and spider-webbed glass, she watched his figure blur and stretch and bend into the shape of a big, dark brown bear. His clothing ripped away into shreds. A huge paw crashed through the window, easily breaking the weakened glass with a ear-splitting crash. Not finished, the bear growled and fumbled at the door, finally ripping the entire thing off of the mangled car and throwing it away into the slushy snow. Cold air swirled into the car, and she crawled carefully over the broken glass towards the bear, grateful for her sturdy jeans and coat.

He was human by the time she had wiggled her way to the door, and strong arms pulled her out the final bit.

"Are you hurt?" he asked anxiously, holding her closer than was strictly necessary.

"My ankle," Patricia admitted, and she was amused when Lee shivered; all that remained of his clothing was a puddle of ripped cloth at their feet. Even his boots had been rent from the ferocity of his transformation.

"I can carry you back up to the road," Lee said firmly.

"You're naked," Patricia giggled hysterically, looking at the steep snowy slope up to the road. It was astonishing how far she had rolled in the car. "You don't even have boots."

"Not like this," Lee said, and right under her arms, he shifted again, flowing into his bear form.

This close, right in his arms, it was completely different than watching it through an obscured window or simply waking up to it. His entire mass changed as a thick coat of fur seemed to come from nowhere, growing into long fur under her very fingers. She had to let go of him as he rose above her, and gasped in pain as she put weight onto her bad ankle. As large as the bear had seemed that morning when they met in bed, he was much larger looming right over her on hind legs. He must be eight or nine feet tall, Patricia realized in awe. Then he was dropping to all fours next to her, growling conversationally as he came to lay directly in front of her.

When she hesitated, uncertain, he raised his head and whined like a dog, twitching his massive shoulders at her suggestively.

It was still a rather good climb onto Lee's back, but the long, coarse fur gave her plenty to hold onto. Patricia swung her good foot over the ridge of his back and was astride. Lee gave a growl of warning and surged to his feet. Patricia clung tight, and as he began to climb up the slope, had to lean forward further and further, until she was basically lying against his shoulder, arms reaching as far around the bear's neck as she could. She continued to lie this way once they had leveled out on the road, cheek pressed into his fur. It was surprisingly comforting, riding in this fashion. He smelled like forests and wild things, and oddly just like Lee, and the rough fur felt just right under her fingers. The rhythm of the muscles striding beneath her was reassuring, and the snuffling growling noises he made as he walked were somehow familiar.

For just a moment, she was a princess in the fairy stories, rescued by her very own bear prince.

Then they were at his truck, and he was lying down again so she could dismount, carefully, hopping on her one good foot. She was opening the truck door when he was behind her as a human again, lifting her up onto the creaking bench seat.

"I should take you to the hospital," Lee said, sliding in beside her after a moment.

"You're naked," Patricia reminded him.

"They've probably gotten odder patients at the hospital," Lee said, but he looked embarrassed as well as cold. He cranked up the heat.

"Just take me to your house," Patricia said. "It's a weekend, and they'll only tell me to elevate it and get x-rays Monday when the walk-in clinic is open. It's not an emergency, and I'd rather call the car insurance company from your quiet house than a crowded ER."

LEE GROWLED, BUT DECIDED that Patricia was right. He didn't relish the idea of arriving at the hospital in his current state of undress, and Patricia didn't seem badly hurt. He turned back up the road towards his house rather than continuing into town.

"I'm... sorry I scared you," he said, after a long moment of silence spent squirming on the cold bench, trying to find a way to keep his seatbelt on without it pressing into his chilled flesh.

Patricia shifted on the seat, fumbling with her boots. "You didn't scare me," she said with surprise. "I was glad to see you, and being a bear shifter was particularly useful of you."

Lee could only sputter at that. "Useful?"

"I doubt even you could have torn off that door without a little help," Patricia said. "And while I'm sure I wouldn't have died there, I was getting cold and... alone."

"You're not afraid of the bear part of me," Lee said, puzzled by this reveal.

"You're clearly still *you* as a bear," Patricia said practically. "You were far more interested in helping me get out of the car than you were in, say, eating me."

"But... this morning?" Lee felt thick-headed, like he was missing something critical.

"It was a pretty shocking way to wake up, no doubt," Patricia said. "Is that what you were apologizing for? It's not like I blame you for not telling me earlier. It's a pretty big confession. 'Hi, I'm a bear sometimes.'"

"But you don't mind that I'm a shifter." Lee couldn't wrap his mind around the idea.

Patricia shot him a sheepish smile. "I'm a little envious," she confessed. "It sounds rather wonderful."

Lee chewed on that for a few moments. "Then why did you leave?"

Her stillness radiated unhappiness, and Lee had to force himself to watch the road instead of immediately reaching to comfort her.

He navigated a slippery curve before she finally answered slowly. "It was what you said about soulmates. I... know you still love your wife, that she meant everything to you. I know you'll never feel that way about me, that I can't be *that*." There was a little hitch to her voice that cut Lee to the bone. "I don't want to be that woman who can't separate sex and love, but I couldn't keep loving you the way I do knowing that what we had was just a pale shadow of what you'd had."

Lee slammed the brakes on, pulling the truck into the snowbank by the side of the road with a curse that had Patricia clinging to the handholds and looking at him with saucer eyes. "You thought I was saying that *Angela* was my soulmate?"

Patricia blinked at him. "Of course..."

Lee leaned his face on the steering wheel, cursing again. "I am the biggest idiot in the entire Midwest," he said, refraining from ripping the entire steering wheel off and throwing it out the window in frustration. He took a series of deep breaths, and unpeeled his fingers from the wheel. "I loved Angela," he said, then thought that might be a poor place to start, but it was an important detail. He met Patricia's eyes; they were full of tears. "But what I felt for her, it's no less than what I have in my heart for you. I never believed in soulmates before I met you. I thought it was a comfortable fiction, just a fairy tale."

"Like shapeshifters?" Patricia muttered. She rubbed the tears away from one cheek and Lee had to put a hand against her face and rub the other dry with a tender thumb.

"When I saw you, I knew it was all the truth. You were meant for me. Every part of me loves every part of you."

Patricia sobbed, but her face lit up behind the tears. "I never believed in love at first sight," she said in a small voice. "And I thought you couldn't possibly feel that way about me..."

Lee unclipped his seatbelt and fought free of the frigid contraption so he could slide across the benchseat and scoop her into his arms. She escaped her own seatbelt to meet him halfway, and lifted her mouth for his kiss with the same hunger that was coursing through his veins. Cold as he was, he burned for this woman, his perfect mate.

Their kiss was a tangle of tongues and a release of fears and despair, deep and long and lingering. If it hadn't been for the gasp of pain that Patricia gave when she moved her foot wrong, Lee was not sure how long they would have stayed there in the frosting truck cab.

Instead, he pulled back, then began cursing again as something occurred to him.

"What is it?" Patricia asked in alarm.

"Your ring," Lee told her. "It was in my pocket, and must be back with my ruined clothing at your car."

"My... ring?"

"Will you marry me?" It wasn't even close to the way he had planned to ask her. "You're mine, and I want everyone to know it."

The glowing smile she gave him, and the kiss that followed was answer enough.

# Chapter Twenty

PATRICIA GAVE LEE HER parka to get into the house; he wrapped it inelegantly around his waist as an attempt at modesty. Both Andrea and Clara seemed more bothered by the way that Patricia was limping than by Lee's state of undress.

Andrea, to Patricia's surprise, was wrapped in Lee's oversized clothing. She looked between them, more puzzled than suspicious. There had been no other vehicle in the drive. "You're a shifter, too?" she guessed.

Andrea grinned. "You always said I had eyes like a hawk."

Patricia groaned. "This explains so much."

"Clara and I are making cookies," Andrea said with a nod towards the stairs. "I think Patricia needs a detailed checkover," she suggested. "Make sure she doesn't have any scrapes she doesn't know about."

Clara thought that was a fine idea, and brought Lee a first aid kit from the downstairs bathroom that he slung over one shoulder.

"You should both take a hot shower, too," Andrea suggest unsubtly. "To warm up, you know. We'll be down here making cookies for a long time. Don't rush, or anything."

Patricia could only sputter helplessly at the suggestion, but Lee seemed to think it was a perfect idea. "I want to check your head for lumps," he said, tightening the parka around his waist.

Then he swept her up into his arms over her protests, and carried her up the stairs.

"Have fun!" Andrea called up after them.

Patricia thought she would be too embarrassed to do anything, aware that Andrea was downstairs knowing exactly what was happening, but when Lee put her gently down on the wide ledge of his bathtub, nothing else seemed to matter.

He shed the parka so that his check-over of her was done entirely nude, and took his duties very seriously, undressing her slowly and looking over every inch of skin as it was exposed. The cuts from glass, all minor, were gently cleaned and antibiotic cream was applied. The bandages Lee had were all princess-themed, and carefully applied over a handful of abrasions. He explored her skull with probing fingers that lingered in her hair more than strictly required. Together they found a few tender spots, but no rising lumps.

"You're going to have a black eye," he informed her, sweeping her hair back from her face.

"I don't have to look at me," Patricia said, aware that her smile must look foolish.

"You'll still look beautiful to me," Lee said with a kiss.

The kiss only delayed their first aid for a moment, then it was time for the part that Patricia was dreading. He pulled her first boot off carefully, and the second even more cautiously. It hurt, but not as badly as Patricia had feared it would. The ankle was angry and swollen, but she could, at his insistence, move it through its entire range. Lee bound it up snugly with a bright pink stretch-bandage, and helped Patricia carefully wriggle out of her jeans to complete their inspection. There would be bruises where the seatbelt had kept her in the seat. "I should probably stay out of swimsuit competitions for a few weeks," she joked, poking at one of the bruises that was already starting to purple.

"You were lucky," Lee said grimly. There was a scowling ferocity to him that Patricia now recognized was driven by his grumpy bear.

"It's passed," she soothed him, caressing his shoulders. "I'll be fine, just forget it."

Lee responded, his nudity making his sudden arousal apparent. "Forget what?" He lifted her up into his arms again, and carried her to the bed. They were both still chilled, and he swept the comforter up over them and dove in. Wrapped in its warmth and darkness, they explored each other's bodies blindly. Lee was surprisingly delicate for his size, taking painstaking care not to jostle her ankle.

It took only moments of delicious discovery to warm up and thrust the blanket off, and Lee gently kissed her from jaw to naval, then straddled her, his erect penis promising unspoken pleasure. When he hesitated, Patricia pulled him down onto her, careful to keep her injured foot out of the way. His entrance claimed her, and her heart sang when she remembered that he felt for her as she did him.

Soulmates. *Mates.*

They were perfect partners, and they fit together like interlocking puzzle pieces, entwining as only two things destined for each other could.

His touch made every square inch of her skin burn for him. He drew her up to heights of pleasure she'd never known or even imagined, then fell with her in the warm afterglow.

Later, in a haze of sated exhaustion, Patricia let Lee tuck her under the comforter with her foot propped up on a pillow. She fell asleep to the smell of cookies and the sound of a shower running.

When she woke a short time later, she found herself alone. There was a glass of water on the bedside table, and a few over-the-counter pain pills that she gratefully took. A package lay on the other side of the bed, wrapped with a paper bag and tied with what appeared to be a sash from one of Clara's dresses. A cane leaned against the side of the bed.

Curious, Patricia unwrapped the crinkly package, and unfolded a length of fuzzy material, printed all over with pink kittens and mittens. A small black box fell out of the folds, and she scooped it up with trembling hands. It opened with a snap and revealed a sparkling ring, with rubies and diamonds flush to an intricate braid of multi-colored gold. She pulled it out of the velvet case and slipped it carefully onto her ring finger, marveling at the fit and sparkle and grinning fit to split her face. For some foolish reason, she wanted to cry, and to distract herself, she turned to inspect the cloth it had been wrapped in. It took her a moment to figure out what it was, and when she did, she burst out laughing.

Andrea laughed as well, when Patricia made her way down to the kitchen wearing both gifts and limping on the cane. "Is that a pair of footed kitty pajamas?"

Lee insisted that Patricia sit down at once, and fussed over elevating her foot. Clara brought her an ice pack from the freezer and carefully perched it onto the ankle, while Andrea brought a plate full of cookies.

"Where on earth did you find these?" Patricia asked Lee. She felt like she was wrapped in downy feathers, the fabric was so soft and fuzzy, and she was deeply cozy and warm. Was this what being a bear felt like?

"It was a special order," Lee said, smiling at her from across his own plate of cookies. "My tailor thought I was nuts, but he put it together anyway."

"I love it," Patricia said, deeply content. Looking around the kitchen, at Clara's eager face, her best friend's laughter in the air and her mate looking at her with love and adoration, she could not imagine a happier ending in any fairy tale ever.

# Epilogue

"I'M NOT USED TO HAVING anyone take care of me," Patricia confessed, letting Lee pile pillows under her ankle. "It's not even broken."

Lee scowled at her, a dear, familiar expression. "It's sprained," he said fiercely. "And you aren't staying off of it at preschool!"

"I make Andrea do most of the work," Patricia promised, touched by his care.

"How was it?" Lee asked. "Really, are you careful?"

Patricia put a hand over his, and was caught by the still-unexpected sparkle of gems on her finger. "I really do take it easy," she laughed. "And things are going smoothly. The new car handles great. Harriette is still missing and Trevor's living with his Dad now. That was half my stress!"

She was rewarded by an easing of the lines in his face, and then Clara was scampering into the living room, carrying a tray with a variety of Lincoln Logs on it. "I baked you cookies!" the little girl announced, and she solemnly gave one to each of them, and then took them back, declaring, "They have to cook more now."

She was gone as quickly as she'd come in, and Patricia exchanged an amused look with Lee that faded to alarm as something occurred to her. "Should I be worried about Clara turning into a bear cub some day at preschool?" she demanded. She couldn't imagine explaining that one away at storytime.

Lee shook his head. "Some shifters are born shifting, but my family has always come into it at puberty. It varies."

Patricia raised an eyebrow at him. "As if puberty weren't complicated enough," she said wryly.

"Are you reconsidering?" Lee gave her ring a tap.

Patricia gave him a searching look, trying to decide if he was really worried, or if he was just teasing her. She smiled. "You can't scare me off that easily."

"I'll have to try harder," Lee said with a sigh, and Patricia knew he was needling her.

"I can't imagine you being harder than you were last night," she whispered suggestively.

He grinned back. "I'm sure I can *rise* to the challenge."

## A note from Zoe Chant

Thank you for buying my book! I hope you enjoyed it as much as I enjoyed writing it.

If you'd like to be emailed when I release my next book, please visit my webpage at zoechant.com and ask to be added to my mailing list. You are also invited to join my VIP Readers Group on Facebook for sneak previews and chats.

Please keep reading for a special sneak preview of *The Tiger Next Door*!

Cover art © Can Stock Photo, design by Layla Lawlor

# Sneak Preview: The Tiger Next Door

"Mr. Powell?"

Shaun rubbed his face and reminded himself that glowering at the intercom was ineffective. "What is it?" he asked shortly.

"It's Mrs. Powell ... Er, Mrs. ex-Powell... Ah..."

"Harriette."

"Yes, Mr. Powell."

Shaun momentarily wished his office had an escape exit. Wasn't there some sort of requirement for that kind of thing? But they were dozens of floors up, looking out over Minneapolis, and vanishing out the window to scale a fire escape was unlikely to happen. Why couldn't he have a more useful shifted form, he wondered. Something that could *fly*.

His inner tiger gave an unamused snort.

"Mr. Powell?"

"Send her in."

Shaun had been expecting... something. A phone call? A demand for more money?

He hadn't been expecting Harriette to visit at his office.

And he definitely wasn't expecting the little boy who was holding her hand.

*Trevor*.

Whatever regrets he had about his brief and stormy marriage to Harriette, Trevor had never been one of them.

Trevor must be five now, and Shaun had seen him just twice in the past two years: awkward visits on his birthday. Trevor had been understandably shy and confused about him, and Shaun went away wondering if it wasn't kinder to step back and let him build a healthy relationship with whatever partner Harriette had last found to replace him.

He scowled and returned his gaze to Harriette. She must have some wild demands if she was dragging Trevor in for leverage.

"What can I do for you?" he asked. It *must* be money.

"I'm not here to ask you for anything," Harriette said, in that terribly reasonable tone she'd always had. "I'm here to give you what you keep asking for."

Shaun scrambled to think of anything he'd asked for since the divorce. His lawyer had tried to convince him to fight harder against her ridiculous financial demands, but Shaun had only wanted one thing — and Harriette's lawyer had been able to get *her* full custody of their son. His work and hours were 'incompatible' with raising a child.

"This is about the house in Green Valley?" Shaun guessed. "I got the foreclosure warning. I'm not sure how you bypassed the fund I set up to pay for that. Did you think it wouldn't count towards child support this way?"

"Don't be stupid," Harriette said. That was the Harriette from the end of their marriage. The cutting one who had already found something better to move on to. "I'm bringing you Trevor."

Shaun wasn't sure who to stare at.

Trevor was gazing at the fishtank, ignoring his parents' conversation. His blond hair was several shades lighter than Shaun's. Harriette had taken to dyeing her hair the same shade as Trevor's instead of her natural brunette, which was downright eerie.

Harriette put the papers she was holding down on Shaun's desk and plucked a pen from his holder. "I had my lawyer draw up the papers. You wanted him, you got him."

Shaun glanced at Trevor, his heart hurting for the boy. How brutal could it be, hearing Harriette give him away like he was nothing?

Trevor didn't seem to notice, staring enraptured at the fish.

Shaun stood and drew Harriette as far away from Trevor's hearing as the office could manage. "You mean you found someone new and he's an impediment? What happened to the real estate guy who loved kids?"

"That's none of your business," Harriette hissed. "Just sign the papers. It's what you want anyway."

Shaun stared at her, trying to remember that he'd found her beautiful once. She was so strong-willed and sure-footed, with her perfect make-up and sultry smile. Shaun only now really realized how much of that was an act.

She had never really wanted Shaun, only the successful investment company he was building. And once she'd set her sights on him, Shaun hadn't stood a chance.

"What about the house in Green Valley?"

Harriette shrugged. "I don't care. Trevor's got some stuff left there."

How had he thought she was sensitive and sweet?

"I go to preschool in Green Valley," Trevor said shyly, joining them.

Harriette ignored him. "Are you going to sign it or not?"

"Do you like your preschool?" Shaun asked gently.

Trevor seemed to perk up. "Yeah! There's a rabbit, and Miss Andrea can juggle. Miss Patricia plays piano."

"It's great," Harriette said dismissively. "Papers?"

"I'm not signing anything my lawyer hasn't looked at," Shaun said firmly.

Harriette's eyes narrowed. "Then I'll take him with me," she threatened. "I'm leaving the country, and with full custody, I don't have to clear that with you."

Shaun's stomach clenched and his tiger growled.

He looked down at Trevor's anxious face, remembering the scant armful he had been as a baby, and the fascinating expressions Shaun had spent so much time gazing at. Trevor had been taking his first steps when Shaun's marriage began to fall apart. After a few months of separation and a divorce that cost him hundreds of thousands of dollars, Harriette had taken their son to the quiet town of Green Valley; in no small part, Shaun knew, because it was just beyond a comfortable commute for visits.

Shaun had lost two years of Trevor's life. He'd gone away a toddler and stood before him now as a little boy. He could almost see the shape of the man he was going to grow up to be in the steady gaze and the set of the chin.

Trevor reached up and began to pick his nose.

"I'll sign," Shaun said quietly.

"Are we going back to Green Valley now?" Trevor asked in concern, looking from Harriette to Shaun. "I don't want to miss preschool."

"*You're* going back to Green Valley," Harriette said dismissively. "I'll be happy never to set foot in it."

She watched in triumph as Shaun read over the contract and signed it. He wasn't a lawyer, but it was a simple document compared to their divorce, and it said what he most wanted to see: full custody. No strings.

Harriette smirked.

"I saw the part about the settlement payment," Shaun growled. "So there's no need to feel smug. I'll have the secretary write you a check on your way out."

It would have been worth twice as much, to have Trevor back.

"What about preschool?" Trevor asked again. "I don't want to miss it. On Monday we're making Easter baskets."

"I... guess we're going to Green Valley, then," Shaun said in bemusement. "We'll check out the house and get it ready to sell and then we can move back here to the city together."

Harriette took her copy of the contract. "Whatever you want," she said dismissively. She gave Trevor a cursory hug. "Don't muss my hair," she warned the boy.

Trevor, realizing something was going terribly wrong, began to cry and cling to her. "I don't want you to go, Mummy. I don't want to live in the city. I want to go to preschool and stay in Green Valley."

Harriette peeled him carefully off. "You're going to live with your daddy now. We talked about this, remember? Be a brave, good boy and say goodbye now."

Trevor, chin trembling, let her go.

And then she was gone, leaving the best thing she'd ever done behind.

"CAN I GET A REFILL?"

Andrea jotted down notes as fast as she could, cursing the fading pen and the textured napkin as she tried to remember the sequence of events she'd figured out while she was waiting for Stanley to pick from the menu that hadn't changed in twenty years.

"Order up!"

Damn. What had she figured out for the villain's motivation? She'd thought of a way to bring the cat back into the plot, hadn't she? She added a few question marks and a scrawl that might have been "cat" and "motivation for villain?" That would hopefully be enough to jog her memory later.

"Order UP!"

Andrea startled. Old George rarely repeated anything he didn't have to. Andrea tucked the pen and napkin into her apron, hoping that it would be readable later.

She swept the food from the kitchen window onto her tray, grabbed the water pitcher with her other hand, and nearly delivered the order to the wrong table.

"Patricia is a better waitress," Marta told her with the candor of someone who was past thinking what people thought of her as she accepted the plate of hash and eggs. "Doesn't this come with toast?"

"Patricia is a much better waitress," Andrea agreed with return frankness. "But she rolled her car and sprained her ankle, and Gran doesn't have much of a hiring pool to draw on, so you're stuck with me for a few weeks." She refilled Marta's water glass without sloshing too much of it onto the laminated tabletop.

Marta laughed with appreciation. "Probably more than a few weeks," she said speculatively. "With her new billionaire boyfriend, she doesn't have to wait tables for us commoners."

"Oh, you know Patricia," Andrea laughed. "She's not suited to being a kept woman. She'll be back at Gran's Grits before you know it, making me look bad again."

Marta kindly did not mention that Andrea was doing a perfectly fine job of looking bad without Patricia's comparison, and Andrea didn't add that she really needed the paycheck and hoped that Lee would convince Patricia to stay off the ankle as long as possible.

Andrea pretended not to see Devon wave his empty glass at her as she scooted back to the window.

"Marta needs toast," she reminded the short order cook.

"Waitress is supposed to do that." George wasn't actually that old, but he shaved his head and had a short, grizzled beard in salt and pepper, and since no one could remember a time without him around, he wore the nickname well. "Did Stanley ever decide?"

"Oh, crap," Andrea said, fishing into her apron pocket. She found two crumpled napkins of notes and an order ticket. "The fish lunch special," she said triumphantly, putting it into George's hand. "No salt on the fries."

"Go give Devon a refill, here's the toast you were supposed to make." George didn't sound happy about it, but Andrea gave him her best 'I'm-an-airhead-please-don't-fire-me' smile and cheerfully marched the toast back to Marta's table.

"What were you drinking?" she asked Devon, taking the glass and straw.

Devon looked at her like she was an idiot. "Iced tea."

"Oh, right. Soda machine's down."

"Maybe write that down on a napkin?" Devon suggested caustically.

Andrea blushed as she stalked away. Since she probably wasn't going to get a tip anyway, she did a second-rate job stirring in the sugar, knowing it would be a gritty sludge at the bottom. Patricia probably stirred it until it was completely dissolved and remembered the lemon every time.

Andrea picked the last, ugly lemon slice from the bowl and tried to position it to look its most hideous.

When she went to refill glasses of water throughout the small, dated diner, the regulars smiled and shook their heads at her.

"How's the book going?" Stanley asked her as she put his fish down in front of him.

"Oh, you know. I've got some ideas. Working away at it." Andrea didn't want to admit that the book was still mostly napkins and notes.

Somehow, when she started writing, tired from a day working at the preschool and an afternoon waiting tables, it didn't seem as captivating as she imagined it would be while she was otherwise busy. And at home, there were dirty dishes waiting for her to wash, and laundry in a heap by the washer, and spring was starting to melt the snow and expose all the things in her yard that needed to be picked up.

Somehow, she managed to instead spend an hour writing instructions to her aunt about unclogging her toilet, with pictures and diagrams, instead of adding actual chapters.

And there was the sky, begging for flight.

"Well, you just remember us, when you're a famous writer," Stanley told her warmly. "You remember Green Valley and all of us who cheered you on."

Andrea smiled and patted his hand, to be rewarded with a largely-toothless smile. "I could never forget," she promised.

Made in the USA
Coppell, TX
31 July 2023

19794666R10069